ARABELLA FINDS OUT

Jaqueline Whitehead

CHRISTIAN FOCUS PUBLICATIONS

© 1996 Jaqueline Whitehead
ISBN 1-85792-161-5

Published by
Christian Focus Publications Ltd
Geanies House, Fearn, Ross-shire,
IV20 1TW, Scotland, Great Britain

Cover design by Donna Macleod
Cover illustration by Elroy Hughes, Allied Artists

Printed and bound in Great Britain by
Cox & Wyman Ltd, Reading, Berks

Contents

Chapter 1

Arabella was rich, very rich. In fact she was very, very, very rich, at least her father was, and that meant she was too. At one time her father had been poor, but he didn't like it very much, so he decided to become rich. He did this by buying things that were cheap and nasty and selling them for too much money to anyone who would have them. Things like plastic Big Bens that played 'Maybe it's because I'm a Londoner', which were very popular with Japanese tourists, and solar powered torches which were a big hit with Eskimos. Strangely enough, even by selling things like these he became rich very quickly and by the time Arabella was born he had quite forgotten what it felt like to be poor.

By the time Arabella was six she was quite used to telling off the servants, being rude to the gardeners and ordering Hargreaves the chauffeur to drive through enormous puddles, just after he had spent all morning waxing the Bentley.

Arabella didn't go to school but had a private tutor called Miss Marshall who came to the house on Mondays, Tuesdays, Thursdays and Fridays. On those days Arabella would go upstairs to the school room for her lessons. These were not a great success because when Miss Marshall said, 'Good Morning, Arabella, please open your books,' Arabella would shout, 'No! go and buy me some sweets.'

When Arabella was nine her mother said to her one morning at breakfast, 'Darling, I think it's time you went to school.'

'What!' said Arabella.

'Don't say what,' said her father, his mouth full of buttered croissant and French coffee, 'Say pardon.'

Arabella glared at her father and shouted, 'What! What, what, what, what, what!' and pulled a face at him. Then she shrieked at her mother, 'I don't want to go to school, I want to stay at home with Miss Marshall.'

'Miss Marshall is not a very good teacher,' said her mother. 'What is three and three?'

'Eight!' yelled Arabella.

'Good grief!' said her father. 'It's definitely time you went to school.' He was good at sums because he was used to counting all his money. He smiled at his wife. 'Have you a school in mind, my dearest?'

'Yes I have,' she replied. 'Lady Worthington's Educational Establishment for rich, genteel young ladies.'

'Sounds ideal,' said Arabella's father. 'Why not give them a call after breakfast?'

'I did think we might take a drive over there this morning and have a chat with the head,' suggested Arabella's mother.

'Even better,' said Arabella's father warmly. 'It is Hargreaves's day off but I could drive us, it would make a pleasant change.'

'That's settled then,' said Arabella's mother, 'I'll go and get ready.'

'I don't think we had better take "you-know-who" this time, do you?' said Arabella's father, nodding at Arabella in a very obvious way, but one which he clearly believed she wouldn't notice. Arabella's mother agreed completely with the wisdom of this.

'We won't take you this time, Snookums,' he said to Arabella, 'you can come and see your new school the next time we go.'

'Dadsy...' Arabella spoke in a soft wheedling tone. 'Snookums doesn't want to go to school.'

'I know,' he replied. 'But I'm afraid this time Snookums will have to trust that Mumsy and Dadsy know best.'

Arabella reverted to her old self.

'I don't want to go to school! I don't want to go to school! I don't want to go to school! I don't! I don't! I don't!' she screamed. After yelling blue murder for three minutes, holding her breath until she turned grey and threatening to be sick Arabella gave up, realising this time Mumsy and Dadsy had made up their minds. How they must hate her to make her leave home every day to go to school.

Arabella flounced off, feeling very cross and frustrated. No one understood her, no one cared, she didn't matter. As these thoughts took hold of her, she began to feel very sorry for herself. Two big tears rolled down her cheeks and she stopped flouncing and became like a heroine in a tragedy. Suddenly with dramatic affect she flung an arm across her face and ran sobbing to the summer house in the east gardens, hoping all the way that someone would see her performance and come to comfort her. There she threw herself to the floor and gave in to what she hoped was 'abandoned sobbing'. Arabella had read about it in a romantic book she'd found in Miss Marshall's bag when she was looking for peppermints, and liked the sound of it. Miss Marshall never did find out where her book had gone, nor the peppermints for that matter.

Arabella sobbed as loudly as she could, hoping all the time that her parents would hear and realise how cruel they were being, but instead she heard the car start at the front of the house and pull away down the drive.

She stopped sobbing. What a cheek, they hadn't even come to say goodbye! She pouted sorrowfully, 'I'm all alone, with no one to care for me.' She said the words out loud and liked the feel of them. In fact there was a house full of staff, so she wasn't alone at all, but the thought suited Arabella's mood. At this she considered another bout of abandoned sobbing but there was no one around to appreciate it. Instead she hauled herself up off the floor on to the wooden seat that ran round the inside of the summer house. Now what was she going to do? It was ages until lunch and she was bored already.

Arabella looked out of the summer house window across the gardens. In the distance she saw the sturdy timber fence that marked the east boundary of her family's property. She could see, too, the outline of a five-bar gate that she knew opened into a wood, with the village less than half a mile further on. Arabella had never gone through that gate and she found herself wondering what it would be like to walk through and down to the village, all on her own. She had never done that either, but always went in the Bentley, driven by Hargreaves.

As Arabella sat looking at the gate she had an idea. 'I know, I'll run away! I will! I'll run away through that gate into those woods and I expect I'll be eaten by bears! They'll soon wish they had never suggested school.' She stood up and in a very determined fashion strode out of the summer house and across the gardens heading towards the trees.

'The woods' wasn't a very accurate term for the little copse that stood just on the other side of Arabella's fence. Once, many years before, it had been part of a great forest that stretched across the countryside, but over the years this had been gradually cut away to make room for the village as it grew. Now there were little more than three or four rows of trees, with thin, stubbly undergrowth. In spite of this, as Arabella came nearer to it, she began to feel afraid. Her imagination caused the trees to grow huge and forbidding, and she tried hard to remember if Miss Marshall had ever taught her about whether there were still bears in England or not.

By the time she reached the gate, she'd decided running away was not such a good idea after all, and that she would rather have a drink and a doughnut instead.

She turned to go back. It was then she heard a voice, causing her to jump violently and squeal with fear.

'Who's there? Who is it?' she squeaked nervously, wishing with all her heart she hadn't come so far.

'It's only us,' said the voice. 'Sorry if we made you jump.'

'Who are you and what do you want?' Arabella looked but could see nothing, then looking harder she realised there were two people hidden in the shadows of the wood, both so grubby and dirty they were almost the same colour as the trees.

'My name's Mary,' said the taller one, 'and this is my brother Fred. I'm nine and he's seven.'

'What are you doing here?' said Arabella, becoming cross, which sometimes happens when you've had a fright.

'We like to come and look at the big house. Do you live there?' They walked out into the daylight, so Arabella could see them properly.

'Yes I do and you shouldn't stand and stare at it.'

'Why not?'

'Because it's my house and I say so. Come over here,' she pointed at the gate.

'Why should we?' said Mary defiantly.

'Because I say so,' said Arabella again.

'Oh all right.' The girl opened the gate and both children walked through. They stood smiling at Arabella, who stared back at them.

'Aren't you dirty?' remarked Arabella, who really had very few good manners.

'Yes. We always are on a Saturday,' said Mary. 'We have to be clean from Sunday to Friday, so we like to get nice and dirty on a Saturday, which is today.'

'Why do you have to be clean from Sunday to Friday?' asked Arabella.

'Well, we go to school Monday to Friday, and Sunday School on a Sunday, so we have to look respectable, as Dad puts it. Mum doesn't call Saturday Saturday any more, she calls it "Dirtyday", 'cos of us,' Fred chuckled.

'I've got to go to school soon,' said Arabella sadly.

'Don't you go now then?' asked Mary.

'No, I'm taught at home by a private tutor.'

'Phew!' whistled Mary.

'Phew!' whistled Fred. He had just learnt how to whistle after months of trying and was very pleased with himself. 'Isn't that a bit dull, with no friends round you?'

'Not at all,' said Arabella snootily. 'Anyway where do you go to school?'

'In the village,' said Mary. 'It's not very big, but it's nice. Where are you going?'

'To Lady Worthington's Educational Establishment for rich, genteel young ladies.'

'Phew!' whistled Mary.

'Phew!' whistled Fred. 'You must be very rich.'

'Yes, I am,' said Arabella. 'Are you?'

'No,' said Mary, matter-of-factly. 'Not at all.'

'How awful!' said Arabella. 'I'd hate to be poor.'

'We're not poor,' countered Mary. 'We're just not rich.'

'Same thing,' said Arabella.

''Tis not,' said Mary.

''Tis!' said Arabella. 'Have you got a pony?'

'No,' said Mary.

'Have you got your own bathroom next to your bedroom?'

'No.'

'Have you got a swimming pool and a tennis court and your own cinema?'

'No.'

'Then you're poor,' said Arabella.

'No I'm not!' said Mary becoming indignant. 'I live in a very nice house and have a very nice life.'

'But you're not rich!' said Arabella.

'Not the way you mean,' replied Mary.

'Ha! Then you're poor!' said Arabella triumphantly.

'I am not poor!' Mary's patience ran out and she gave Arabella a hard push. Fred laughed.

'You pushed me and he laughed,' shrieked Arabella. 'I'm going to tell my mummy and daddy and they'll have you arrested and put into prison for assault and I will stand up in court and say it was all because I told the truth, that you're poor!'

'And you're stupid,' said Mary, a little unsure of herself and a bit worried in case Arabella was right and could have her sent to prison. She turned to go.

'Come on Fred.' Arabella had never had anyone call her stupid before and didn't quite know what to do, but she wasn't so stupid that she didn't realise she had enjoyed talking to Mary and Fred and wanted to continue the conversation.

'Don't go,' said Arabella. 'I want to talk with you.'

'Well, I don't think we want to talk with you, do we, Fred?' said Mary.

'No!' said Fred, though he didn't move. Mary took Fred's hand and they started back through the gate.

'Would you like to come and see my swimming pool?' said Arabella suddenly.

'You've got a swimming pool?' Mary stopped and looked back. 'A real one?'

'Yes,' said Arabella. 'A really enormous one, nearly as big as the ones you see them racing in on television.'

'I don't believe you,' said Mary.

'Come and have a look then,' said Arabella.

'Won't your Mum and Dad mind? We aren't rich you know.'

'I know,' said Arabella with a not-very-nice smile on her face, 'they don't mind what I do as long as I'm happy.' She knew this wasn't exactly true, but it was near enough. 'Anyway they're out.' Arabella began to walk away. Mary and Fred looked across the gardens to the house that stood huge and impressive and then at each other.

Mary swallowed nervously. 'Are you sure no one will mind?' she called out.

'Quite sure,' said Arabella, pleased at the effect she was having on the two children. 'Come on!' Mary and Fred hesitated a moment longer then ran to catch her up. As they walked Fred looked around at the beautiful big garden and whispered, 'Is this a park?'

'Don't know,' Mary whispered back. Arabella overheard and laughed a very loud put-on sort of laugh.

'Now who's stupid, this is my garden, well, part of it anyway, the side part, the front is round there.'

Arabella waved her hand grandly in the direction of the house. 'Round the back is where we grow fruit and vegetables, or rather where Barker the gardener grows them for us; behind that are the tennis courts. The swimming pool is on the other side of the house. Then if you go through a gate and down a little path you come to where the stables are and the paddock where my pony lives.

'Oh,' said Mary breathlessly, not quite able believe what she was hearing and for the first time in her life she felt dizzy with envy.

With some trepidation Mary and Fred followed Arabella through the grounds until they arrived at a wrought-iron gate, which had the outline of a dolphin set into the metalwork. Here Arabella stepped to one side and allowed them to go first. Mary and Fred went through and gasped at what they saw. A lovely oval-shaped pool lay before them, blue and crystal clear. It had its own small diving-board at one end and graceful shallow steps leading down into the water at the other. Round the pool were several reclining chairs and tables. The chairs were padded and lined with a soft colourful fabric that matched the parasols in the centre of each table. The fencing that enclosed the area was a glamorous trellis with climbing plants cleverly trained to grow in and out and over the wood.

'It's like in the films,' said Mary, quite overcome. She and Fred both looked at Arabella with growing respect, this was what it meant to be truly rich.

'Yes it is nice isn't it. You don't have a swimming

pool, do you? It must be awful to be poor.' Arabella noticed with pleasure that Mary didn't argue back this time. 'Come along I've got lots more to show you.'

The next hour flew by as Arabella took Mary and Fred on a tour of her home. She showed them round the vast gardens with their great stretches of lawn dotted with shrubs and flower beds. She showed them the summer house and the ornamental pond full of the biggest goldfish Mary and Fred had ever seen. She showed them the tennis courts and told them about André the tennis coach who came to give her private lessons. Then she took them to the paddock and introduced them to Pixie, a beautiful grey Welsh mountain pony who was, in Arabella's words, 'My very own and the best pony in the world'. Her voice became softer as she spoke about her beloved pet and Mary, who also adored horses and had riding lessons when her parents could afford it, realised Arabella truly loved Pixie.

The tour continued with an inspection of the house, Arabella loudly pointing out all the luxurious features. Mary and Fred were stunned to discover that Arabella had, if not exactly her own cinema, then a study-type of room with a giant screen television at the front; the walls were lined with video tapes.

Finally, they came to Arabella's bedroom. Here Mary's envy reached unbearable proportions. Her own bedroom at best could be described as cosy. Small and compact, with cupboards and a wardrobe not really big enough, so that things were always spilling out. The quilt on her bed was a patchwork one made by her

15

Grandmother and Mary loved it, but nothing she had could compare with what met her eyes now.

Arabella's bedroom was as big as Mary and Fred's dining room and sitting room put together. It was decorated in soft peach and pale green. The bed, a four-poster, was carefully draped in a warm, glowing satin material. One wall could not be seen at all, it was entirely lined with wardrobes and cupboards, and in the centre, cunningly fitted, was a very grown-up-looking kidney-shaped dressing-table, Mary fell instantly in love with it. The door on the opposite wall led into an *en suite* shower and bathroom, all in the same colour scheme. Mary and Fred were now speechless.

Arabella was as pleased as punch. It had all gone better than she could have ever hoped for. These silly village children standing there scruffy and dirty, wishing they had everything she had. Arabella knew they were, and it made her feel important, she found she liked the feeling very much indeed. All her other friends were as rich or richer than she was and though she quite liked some of them, none made her feel so grand as Mary and Fred did.

The truth was Arabella didn't have any proper friends; not surprisingly she didn't get along with other people very well and any children that did come to play, soon got tired of her and asked to go home.

'I want a drink,' said Arabella suddenly. She pressed a button on the bedroom wall and a minute or two later a young woman appeared dressed in black with a white apron. 'Three lemonades and a plate of cakes and don't take all day about it.'

'Yes Miss.' The maid, for that is what she was, said 'Miss', but she didn't look as if she meant it; it was clear she was none too pleased with Arabella's tone of voice, but turning to go she saw Mary and Fred and smiled kindly at them.

'I know you,' said Mary. 'You go to our church, don't you?'

'That's right Miss.'

'Oh, you don't have to call me Miss; I'm Mary and this is my brother Fred.'

'Hello Fred, my name's Lydia,' said the maid. Fred just smiled shyly.

Arabella wasn't too pleased the way things were going. 'When you've quite finished chatting,' she said haughtily, 'go and get our drinks and cakes or I might have to tell my mother and father about you.'

Lydia glared at Arabella but said nothing. She smiled again at Mary and Fred. 'See you both on Sunday?'

'Yes, you will,' replied Mary.

'That's good. I'll be back with your drinks in a moment.'

'Take them down to the pool,' Arabella ordered, 'we will have them there.'

Lydia left the room and Arabella, Mary and Fred went downstairs, back out into the garden and round to the swimming pool. They lay down on the reclining chairs. A few moments later, Lydia arrived with a tray. On it were three glasses of pink-coloured lemonade. Mary and Fred were delighted to see ice floating on the top and that each glass had a brightly-coloured straw and a paper parasol. The plate of cakes looked delicious, too. There was enough for the children to have two each, three ring doughnuts and three chocolate éclairs.

'About time,' snorted Arabella. 'Why have we only two cakes each?'

'That is all Cook would send,' said Lydia.

'I don't believe you. I see I shall have to have a word with my parents, this just isn't good enough. You can go now.'

Lydia's face coloured red and she looked unhappy, but as she walked away she smiled and winked at Mary and Fred, who both waved.

'Why do you speak to her like that?' asked Mary. 'It doesn't sound very nice.'

'You don't have to be nice to staff. If you are, they soon get ideas above their station.'

'What does that mean?' said Mary.

Arabella didn't actually know, but she had heard her parents say it and it sounded grown-up and grand. 'Oh, have your drink, the ice is melting,' she said sullenly. Ten minutes later the plate and glasses were empty.

'We shall have to go soon,' said Mary.

'Oh, do you have to?' responded Arabella. 'I was just beginning to enjoy myself.'

'Yes we shall. Mum will soon start wondering where we are. Thank-you for a lovely time though.' Mary suddenly thought of something, 'We don't even know your name yet.'

'Arabella,' said Arabella. 'The Honourable Arabella Fitzgerald.'

'Oh!' said Mary impressed. 'What a wonderful name. Better than mine, I'm plain Mary Cook.'

'How awful,' agreed Arabella. 'Will you come and see me again?'

'I don't know,' said Mary doubtfully. 'I don't think we are posh enough to be your friends.'

'Maybe not, but I do want you to come and visit me sometimes.'

'We could do that, couldn't we, Fred?' Fred nodded hard, thinking of the lemonade and cakes.

'Next time bring your swimming things, we could go in the pool. I could have Pixie saddled too and you could watch me ride, I might even let you have a go.' This last idea convinced Mary totally.

'Oh, that would be wonderful! More wonderful than you can ever know.'

'Good. What about tomorrow?'

'Can't tomorrow, we go to church.'

'The next day?'

'Can't, we go to school.'

'Oh yes,' said Arabella, remembering school. 'Next Saturday?'

'Yes, we could come next Saturday.'

'Good. Come at ten o'clock sharp, don't be late and don't go to the front door. Come round here, I will be waiting for you.'

'Okay. Goodbye, Arabella, see you next week and thank-you again. Oh!' said Mary stopping suddenly and looking sheepish, 'I'm sorry I pushed you earlier.'

Arabella didn't know what to say to this so she just said, 'Bye', and walked away into the house, without waiting to see them go. Mary and Fred tore off across the garden, scrambled over the fence and ran through the trees towards home. They couldn't wait to tell their mother about their exciting morning.

Arabella walked slowly up to her bedroom. She sat down at the kidney-shaped dressing table and picked up a hair brush. Mary and Fred's visit had given her a good idea and she wanted to think about it a bit more. She knew that Lady Worthington's Educational Establishment for rich genteel young ladies would have girls just as rich as she was, maybe even richer. It would be much more fun to go to the village school where she would be the richest person and where everyone would be jealous of her.

She sat brushing her hair imagining many visits like Mary and Fred's. She thought of tea parties, with boys and girls sitting silent in amazement at all they saw around them. In her mind's eye Arabella could just see their faces growing green with jealousy, and then, of course, they would have to do as they were told so that she would allow them little treats. The idea appealed to her so much that she giggled and rocked back on the chair.

Mumsy and Dadsy might prove a problem if they had set their hearts on Lady Worthington's but Arabella was convinced she could change their minds. She would scream until she was sick if need be. Arabella wasn't sure if she could actually do that, but it might be fun to try. Mumsy and Dadsy must allow her to go to the village school, they mustn't be allowed to spoil her plans.

Arabella sat gloating at her own cleverness, until a bell rang downstairs announcing that it was time for lunch. She made her way to the dining room. Oh good, there were strawberries and cream for pudding.

Chapter 2

Arabella was on her way to the village school. She'd managed to persuade her parents to let her go, although it hadn't been easy. They had very much liked the look of Lady Worthington's Establishment.

The Headteacher had personally taken them on a tour of the school and the more they saw and heard, the more impressed they became. 'Girls from some of the finest families in the land are pupils here,' gushed the Headteacher, 'and we have a number from overseas too: daughters of diplomats, ambassadors and such like. The girls can attend as day pupils or as boarders and as Arabella lives so near, you have the choice.'

There were all the usual lessons at Lady Worthington's but much of the time was given over to classes for things like elocution and deportment. Arabella's parents were shown into a room with a group of girls walking around with books on their heads; there seemed to be a lot of giggling.

'What fun,' commented Arabella's mother.

'Oh yes!' enthused the Head. 'We pride ourselves on having a high element of fun at Lady Worthington's, oh, along with academic excellence of course. In the next room is a class for "How to cope with a bad hair day when your hairdresser's on holiday", most important, I'm sure you will agree.'

They were introduced to the Head girl who was, whispered the Headteacher, connected with royalty. Arabella's parents looked impressed and Arabella's mother wondered if she should curtsy, in the end she decided probably not. By the time they had finished their tour, Arabella's parents were thrilled and delighted with what they had seen and shook the Headteacher's hand warmly.

'How soon can Arabella start?' they enquired.

'As soon as she likes,' the Head gave a carefree wave of her hand. 'Shall we go to my office, we can discuss the details, fees and so on. This way.'

After all that and a good lunch at Luigi's, Arabella's parents were not at all pleased to come home and find their daughter talking enthusiastically about attending the local village school.

'But darling...'

Arabella put her fingers in her ears and hummed loudly.

'But darling...'

Arabella shook her head and screamed, 'No! No! No!'

'But darling...' Arabella jumped up down, then ran around the room singing, at the top of her voice. In the end she didn't actually make herself sick but almost did and then had a sore throat for three days because of all the screaming.

It had been worthwhile though because she had got her own way and now here she was sitting in the back of the Bentley being driven by Hargreaves to the first day at her new school.

Arabella looked down at the clothes she was wearing, it wasn't a uniform as such, the village school didn't have a uniform but everyone had to wear something in the school colours, grey and red. She remembered the prospectus her parents had brought back from Lady Worthington's. The school uniform was a pink and grey track suit with white trainers which were personalised with each girl's own name. Arabella would have loved that.

She thought of the grey sports outfit and black plimsolls in the schoolbag beside her and remembered wistfully the pink and lilac candy stripes on the shorts and T-shirt of the Lady Worthington kit. Never mind it would all be worthwhile when the boys and girls at the village school saw her arrive in the Bentley driven by a chauffeur. Wouldn't they go green! She would soon put the teachers in their place. Everyone would be so pleased to have someone like her at their school they would probably allow her to do anything she wanted.

It occurred to Arabella that word had probably already spread about her. On a Saturday four weeks before, Mary and Fred had visited for the second time and Arabella made absolutely certain they were in no doubt about her wealth.

They arrived at ten o'clock sharp as instructed by Arabella and were a good deal smarter and cleaner than on their first visit. Because of this Arabella's mother and father did not mind too much about her playing with village children. Both of them agreed however that Mary and Fred were not the type they wanted their daughter to mix with. It was one thing going to school with them, it was quite another to bring them home to socialise.

After meeting Mary and Fred, Arabella's father had taken her to one side and whispered that perhaps for next Saturday she should ring Major and Lady Grice's daughter, Roberta, and arrange for her to visit. She was a nice little girl, Arabella's father had muttered in her ear, from an old and respected family.

Arabella replied, also in a whisper, that she hated Roberta Grice and never wanted to play with her again. The truth was that within an hour of arriving Roberta had rather summed Arabella up, she called her mean and nasty, a show-off and a stuck-up prig, then pushed her into some bushes. Of course Mary and Fred heard nothing of this whispered conversation and stood smiling while Arabella's father had, as far as they were concerned, nothing more than a quiet word with his daughter.

After that, one pleasant surprise followed another for the two children as the day turned into a most special occasion.

It began with a trip to Pixie's paddock. The gardener's boy had already groomed the pony until she shone and then saddled and bridled her. Arabella mounted and cantered round the paddock, hopping over some of the little jumps that were scattered about. She was obviously very proud of her pet and treated her kindly, not pulling hard on her mouth and patting her often.

Then it was Mary's turn. She rode quietly as if in dream, quite unable to believe she was actually on a pony without having to pay for the privilege. Fred sat on Pixie for a minute or two while Mary led him and though he quite enjoyed it, he wasn't so keen as his sister and was more than happy to hop off.

The three children then made their way to the swimming pool. They changed into their costumes in a chalet which boasted its own spacious cubicles and showers, then they ran out into the sunlight. This was the moment Fred had been waiting for and gave a great whoop of excitement as he ran along the diving board and bombed into the water. Mary and Arabella swam more sedately, up and down, occasionally doing duck dives and trying to stand on their hands. The water was warm and pleasant and Arabella told them she'd had it heated specially. All the time Mary and Fred thought how wonderful it must be to have these things as part of your home. They did their best not to feel envious but found it very hard.

The morning was soon gone and lunchtime arrived. The children showered, dried themselves, got dressed and went indoors. Fred looked wistfully back at the swimming pool while Mary's thoughts were all of a soft grey Welsh Mountain pony.

They ate in the dining room. Arabella wanted it that way so as to impress the children even more. Lunch was delicious. There was roast chicken with stuffing, roast potatoes, beans, courgettes and little button mushrooms, all served with a rich gravy.

'The vegetables come from our own garden,' Arabella informed them proudly. Fred wasn't keen on vegetables so he wasn't impressed and left the courgettes and mushrooms on the plate. For pudding there was knickerbocker glory, which Arabella chose specially. Mary and Fred were both delighted, they couldn't remember eating a more delicious pudding ever.

After lunch there was a film in the video room, a funny one that made Mary and Fred shriek with laughter, while Arabella did her best to remain dignified and would only allow herself the occasional chuckle.

Halfway through, Lydia arrived with drinks and ice-creams and though the children were still rather full from such a good lunch, they somehow managed to squeeze them down.

At the end of the day, two happy children said a special thank-you to Arabella and walked home, dreaming of all they had seen and done. As for Arabella herself, had she been able to forget about her schemes, she would have enjoyed it too. It hadn't occurred to her that the three of them could just be friends together; what mattered was that the two children got caught up in the wonder of living a rich lifestyle. What was simply a happy and enjoyable day for Mary and Fred, Arabella regarded as a triumph. They would definitely go back and tell all their common friends about it and Arabella would be a celebrity even before she started at their dingy little school.

The drive to the village school was a very short one but before leaving Arabella instructed Hargreaves to go the long way round. This was so that their approach would be from the opposite end of the High Street to where the school was. This, in turn, would mean that any children in the playground could see the Bentley coming and have ample time to gather round. This would allow Arabella to make the type of entrance she hoped for.

Her plans worked perfectly. Mary and Fred had indeed been busy telling everyone about their new friend and her wonderful home. The children were quite excited about the Honourable Arabella coming to their school, and even the staff had caught the mood. Of course, it would be bad for the child if too much fuss was made, so they stayed in the staff room, making up reasons for looking out of the window.

The only one unaffected was the Headteacher, Mrs Carlton, a very wise lady who was no more interested in Arabella, than she was in any other of her pupils. She did wonder, though, how Arabella would shape up at her school if the child's life was as grand as the stories surrounding her suggested.

Mary was at the front of a crowd of children looking out for Arabella's car. As the Bentley turned the corner at the far end of the village she called out, 'She's coming! Arabella's coming!'

Chapter 3

The Bentley drew smoothly to a halt outside the village school and Arabella counted to ten, to allow the full effect of her arrival to sink in before nodding at Hargreaves. With a deep sigh of disapproval and a slight shake of his head, he got out of the car and went round to the passenger door. He opened it, then stood to attention as Arabella climbed out.

If she expected applause she didn't get it, but was still well satisfied with the interested expressions on the faces of all the children. She turned to Hargreaves and in a loud voice, so that everyone watching could hear, she said haughtily, 'I am to be collected at 3.30 sharp.'

'Yes, Miss.' With another deep sigh and a raise of his eyebrows, Hargreaves went gloomily back to the driving seat. He started the engine and drove away, muttering to himself about how different things would be if she were his daughter.

Arabella looked round at the gathering of children. 'Who's going to carry my bag for me?' she said grandly. No one moved.

'Carry it yourself!' The voice came from the back of the crowd and a few children sniggered. Arabella ignored the comment and walked sedately into the playground just in time to hear a bell ring.

'What's that?' she asked.

'It's the bell to tell us school is beginning,' said Mary. 'Come on, Arabella, we line up over here, you can stand in front of me.'

'Oh no, they won't expect me to line up with all the other children. I shall just go straight in.' Arabella moved towards the school door.

'Arabella, please line up with Mary and the others,' called the teacher who had been on playground duty. Arabella looked disgusted, but did as she was told. 'I'll sort things out later,' she muttered to Mary.

When the children were standing quietly in neat rows the teacher blew her whistle and all the boys and girls filed into their classes for registration. Arabella went with Mary into a bright, colourful room which had several large tables placed in no particular order. There were chairs set round them. The effect was businesslike, but friendly.

The children went to their chairs but didn't sit down. A lady was already seated at a large desk to the front of the class and she smiled as the children came in.

'Good morning, boys and girls.'

'Good morning, Miss Little,' the class replied in unison.

'You may sit down.'

Chairs legs scraped noisily against the floor as children pulled their seats back and flopped down; a hubbub of chatter filled the room.

'Please, Miss,' It was Mary speaking. 'Arabella is new, it's her first day.'

'Ah yes, Arabella. Welcome to our school. I am your teacher, Miss Little. I expect everything will be strange at first so do ask if you want to know something, I'm sure Mary and the others will look after you,' she looked round at the class expectantly and several children smiled and nodded. 'It is unusual for someone to start school in the middle of a term, but I'm quite certain you will soon fit in.'

'I want to ask something now,' said Arabella, abruptly.

'Yes?' said Miss Little. 'What is it?'

'I don't have to queue up with the other children, do I? In the morning, I mean.'

'Yes, Arabella, you do.'

'Why?'

'Because it is school rules.'

'Rules are made to be broken,' said Arabella in a very grown-up voice. She'd heard her father say it once and liked the sound of it. Some of the children laughed.

'Not in this school they're not!' said Miss Little, stiffly. She wasn't used to pupils answering back and was not pleased. With a gesture that meant the subject was closed, she turned her attention back to the class. 'Now everyone sit quietly while I call registration.'

Arabella hadn't finished. 'Miss Little, you don't understand...'

'I understand perfectly,' Miss Little interrupted. 'Now be quiet, Arabella, and listen for your name.'

'But...' persisted Arabella.

'Arabella! I insist that you are quiet!'

'But...'

'Arabella!'

With this Arabella jumped to her feet and shouted, 'I

want to see the Headteacher. Immediately!'

Miss Little looked stunned for a second or two, but quickly recovered. She stood up very slowly and advanced towards the child, her face set and serious, her voice hard and cold.

'That can be arranged, but first I wish to speak to you outside. Come with me.'

No one heard what was said between teacher and pupil during the next few minutes, even though the children sat quietly, listening as hard as they could. No one had ever spoken to Miss Little like that before and the children couldn't wait to see what would happen next. Mary looked worried.

When they finally came back in to class, Miss Little was her brisk smiling self and Arabella looked like thunder. She went to her desk and sat glaring at the teacher, who took no notice of her whatsoever.

'Right, children, registration.' No one would have guessed, from Miss Little's voice, that anything was wrong. 'Sit up, listen for your names and answer quickly, please.'

Mary was most surprised when Miss Little came to the 'B' names, 'Arabella Brown?' No answer. 'Arabella Brown!' No answer. 'Arabella, when I call your name, you must say "Yes, Miss".'

'All right. All right,' said Arabella, going a little red. Mary put up her hand.

'Yes, Mary?'

'Miss, that isn't Arabella's name; you've got it wrong. Her name is Fitzgerald.'

'Is it, Arabella? Have we made a mistake?'

'No,' said Arabella, grumpily not looking at Mary. Miss Little went back to the register and calling out names.

'You told me your name was Fitzgerald,' Mary was puzzled.

'It was a game, that's all. Just a game. You're so stupid.' She couldn't say she wished with all her heart that her name was Fitzgerald and that she wasn't just Arabella Brown. She had spoken to her parents many times about having it changed but they just told her not to be silly.

Arabella turned her back on Mary, embarrassed at being found out. She had completely forgotten about the made-up name. She was worried too that Mary might ask her about the 'Honourable' bit, as this was also Arabella's invention and she couldn't face having to explain that as well.

The morning didn't go happily for Arabella. She had never been taught to behave nicely or show respect for others, so saying the wrong thing came naturally. She believed that money could buy almost anything and that being rich meant she could say and do what she liked. It simply didn't occur to her that things could or should be any different.

By break-time she had driven the smiling Miss Little into a frenzy, upset her classmates in a dozen different ways and told the school caretaker he needed a hair cut. She spent morning break in Mrs Carlton's office, hearing in no uncertain terms about how children were expected to behave in her school. Arabella came out hot and bad-tempered, and decided maybe she would go to Lady Worthington's after all.

That evening, when she sat down for dinner she told her parents so.

'Oh no you don't!' said her father with an unexpected hard edge to his voice. 'After all the fuss you made about going to the village school and my having to ring up the Headteacher at Lady Worthington's to explain that you wouldn't be coming after all! Don't you tell me you've changed your mind.'

Arabella tried a new tack. 'Dadsy, Snookums isn't happy; surely you want your Snookums to be happy?'

'Snookums should have thought about that in the first place,' said her father, in a tone of voice Arabella had never heard before. She opened her mouth to scream and her father continued quickly, 'And if you are thinking of screaming and holding your breath go ahead; I will have you carried to your room so we can finish our dinner in peace.'

Arabella was stunned into silence; her father had never spoken to her like that before, she must have really made him cross this time.

Arabella went to bed that night very unhappy, not looking forward to the next day at all. She couldn't sleep for thinking about the way things had turned out. What on earth could she do?

An hour later she was still tossing and turning, worried and sleepless. She had plumped her pillows a dozen times but still they felt hard and prickly, she just couldn't get comfortable, no matter which way she turned. Never before had Arabella had a sleepless night. Never before had there been a reason for one.

It was at the point when exhaustion was making her feel fuzzy, that an idea popped into her head. She grabbed at it thankfully. That might just work and if it did she would certainly become the most popular person in her class and in time, maybe, the whole school. She yawned sleepily. In the meantime, let them think she had listened to Mrs Carlton's talk: she would behave as all the other silly children did and when the time was right, well, then they would listen to her.

Arabella had no energy left to think any more and now the matter was sorted out, her pillows became soft and fluffy again, so with a contented sigh she let herself drift off into a deep sleep.

Next morning Arabella lined up with the other children without any fuss at all. She said 'Yes, Miss Little' most politely when her name was called at registration, and did her best to be helpful. Because being helpful was a new concept to Arabella and because she didn't really mean it anyway, she often got it wrong - like the time she grabbed another girl's cardigan to mop up spilled paint.

'Arabella, you should make sure you use an old rag,' said Miss Little patiently, trying to pacify the girl whose cardigan it was.

'It looked like an old rag to me,' said Arabella, sweetly. 'Old rags at my house are nicer than that cardigan anyway.'

Because Arabella did seem to be making some effort, Miss Little did not punish her harshly, but sent her to the cloakroom to wash the cardigan, first in cold water to make sure the paint came out and then in hot soapy water.

Everyone felt that Mrs Carlton's little talk at yesterday's morning break must have had an affect on Arabella and they all breathed a sigh of relief. Arabella didn't think it had affected her at all and found Mrs Carlton a tiresome and difficult woman. In actual fact, it had touched her far more than she herself knew. It was the very first time she'd ever been made to think about getting along with others.

Mrs Carlton recognised that Arabella had lived a very isolated, lonely childhood, with far too much money and attention lavished on her. She knew too, though, that all children, given the right guidance, could turn out well, so she had high hopes for Arabella. Until then, she felt there would probably be some difficult stormy times ahead and so called a staff meeting to prepare everyone, especially Miss Little.

Unaware of all of this, Arabella went out into the playground for morning break. She took with her a small plastic tub. Inside was an apple, cored, peeled and beautifully sliced. It had been prepared by Cook for her elevenses and each piece of apple had been dipped in lemon juice to stop it going brown.

The other children biting into whole apples or munching on crisps or biscuits gathered round.

'Your apple has a brown squashy bit,' said Arabella

to Mary. 'Ugh!'

'I know,' said Mary, 'I just bite a big bite all round it and then throw that piece away; the rest is all right.'

'Doesn't your Cook prepare your apple for you?' enquired Arabella, politely.

Before Mary could reply, a boy standing to one side said, 'Mine does, but only after the maid has polished it and got the butler to inspect it.'

'Oh!' said Arabella impressed.

The children standing round, shouted with laughter, even Mary smiled and the boy walked away with a big grin on his face.

'What's so funny?' asked Arabella.

'He was taking the mickey,' said a tall girl called Charlotte.

'Taking the what?' Arabella asked puzzled.

'The mickey, the mick - you know, he was joking.' Seeing Arabella still didn't understand she added. 'He was making fun of you.'

'Why, what did I say that was so funny?'

'Are you really that rich?' said Charlotte. All the other children went very quiet, this was what they wanted to know. Had Mary and Fred exaggerated? Arabella suddenly realised that here was an opportunity to put last night's idea into action.

'Yes,' she replied boldly, 'I am.'

'Prove it,' said another girl from the back of the group. The crowd of children was steadily growing larger as word of this conversation spread. Arabella knew her chance had arrived.

'All right. Come to tea on Saturday, in fact come to lunch and spend the day with me.'

'What all of us?' said a small boy.

'Yes, if you all want to come. Though maybe not the whole school this time but certainly my class. Yes why not?' she said as if having the idea for the first time, 'I hereby invite my class to spend the day with me on Saturday. Don't forget to bring your swimming things, the pool is lovely at this time of year and should it be a little chilly I can have the water heated. A barbecue would be nice, don't you think?' Arabella said all of this very casually, knowing that the children would be most impressed. At that moment the bell went to signal the end of morning break and Arabella swept into class delighted by the way things had worked out.

After break Miss Little had a difficult job calming her pupils down, as word of Arabella's invitation spread. For the rest of the week the children spoke of little else. All of them could come except for one boy who was going away for the weekend. He begged his parents to change their plans but they flatly refused.

There was great excitement as the children talked about what might happen and what they might do. Mary and Fred were in big demand to tell over and over again about their visit and while Mary seemed reluctant to do so, Fred was delighted. He had never had so much attention before and was thoroughly enjoying himself. At one point he did get a bit carried away and Mary happened to be passing at the time he described the helicopter ride. He clearly felt put out that he wasn't included in next Saturday's invitation but it was for Arabella's class only.

The rest of the school looked on enviously and hoped that one day they might be invited too. Arabella watched all the goings on thrilled and delighted that her plan was working so well. She couldn't wait for the weekend and glowed with anticipation of what was to come.

Chapter 4

Arabella decided to announce her plans for Saturday at the end of breakfast on Thursday morning. Unfortunately, she chose to do this just as her father had taken a large swig of coffee. The shock of it caused the hot drink to go down the wrong way and he choked violently.

Arabella continued calmly laying out her plans as her father's face turned from red to purple, while her mother, the maid and the butler beat him on the back. Then quietly, with a sweet smile on her face she left the dining-room. Her father gasped for air and made movements with his hands that looked rather like he was throttling someone. As soon as he was able, Arabella's father, with her mother trailing in his wake, stormed upstairs to the bedroom where Arabella sat at the dressing table brushing her hair. Things like 'You can't...' and 'I won't let you...' and 'How dare you?' bubbled from his lips.

Arabella had expected this reaction and simply said, 'You have to let me, I've already asked them: if you don't we will lose face in the village.' At this her father went limp and looked helplessly at his wife, she looked back at him and smiled a thin little smile, then shrugged her shoulders and raised her eyebrows as if to say, 'What can I do?'

He turned to Arabella again. 'Two village children

were bad enough – how many can we expect this time?'

'Twenty-eight,' she replied meekly.

'TWENTY-EIGHT! Twenty-eight little monsters running riot on my property? This time Arabella you've gone too far!'

'They aren't monsters and they won't run riot. You have parties for your friends; I want one for mine.'

'How can you call them friends? You've only been at the school five minutes.'

'That's long enough,' she replied sweetly.

'If only you had gone to Lady Worthington's, this would never have happened.'

'It wouldn't need to,' muttered Arabella, under her breath and put a hand over her mouth to stifle a giggle.

'What did you say?' challenged her father.

'Nothing.' Her face became the picture of innocence.

'Yes, you did. Arabella, what's going on here? What are you up to?'

'Nothing.'

'This is your fault,' Arabella's father rounded on his wife who took a step back. 'You have given her too much, she takes us for granted, she takes everything for granted. I'm not surprised we have twenty-eight monsters coming on Saturday, they were invited by the monster who lives here.'

At first Arabella didn't realise he was talking about her but when she did she was shocked, he had never spoken about his Snookums like that before. She knew this time she had made him very cross and for once in her life couldn't think of anything to say. Her silence seemed to irritate her father even more and he stood glaring at her, tense and furious, his fists clenched into tight balls. Finally, with a snort of impatience he turned on his heel and stormed from the room.

Arabella's mother watched him go, with worried eyes. 'I do wish you wouldn't upset him,' she said to Arabella, then she left the room and followed him downstairs. Arabella could hear her muttering. 'I don't know what's got into him these days, I really don't.'

Chapter 5

Saturday morning dawned early for Arabella. There was a lot to do. By eight o'clock she'd had her breakfast, organised the boy who came to clean the swimming pool, told Simpson the butler to set up the barbecue in the pool area, got the gardener's helper to groom Pixie, made sure the latest release in the video world was ready and in the tape player and told Cook there would be about thirty for lunch.

Cook exploded and said she needed more notice than that, but Arabella just replied that she wanted burgers, sausages, chicken drumsticks and steak, with ice cream sodas and strawberries and cream for pudding. She left the kitchen as Cook turned a similar colour to her father at Thursday's breakfast. Arabella herself did very little that morning but run around giving orders. She did however, find time to stop at Pixie's paddock and give the pony three sugar lumps and a kiss on the nose.

By eleven o'clock everything was ready and Arabella was glowing with anticipation of what lay ahead. She was in her bedroom putting the finishing touches to her appearance and had even put a little make-up on for the occasion. She made a mental check of all that was to happen and ran through the programme for the day to make absolutely sure nothing had been forgotten. No, it was all perfect. She was going to make sure her classmates had the day of their lives! By Monday morning Arabella would the most popular person around. In her imagination she saw the rest of the school begging to have a chance to visit as well.

At eleven thirty sharp the front door bell rang announcing the first of her guests. Arabella checked the mirror one last time, then slowly and with what she hoped was great dignity, she descended the stairs.

When she arrived in the hall, the butler and two maids were already ushering the first of the children in. For a few minutes there was hustle and bustle as coats and bags were taken and put away. Arabella went around greeting her visitors. She said things like, 'So glad you could come' and 'Lovely to see you' - things she had heard her parents say to their guests. She also insisted on shaking hands with each of them in turn which caused much amusement and embarrassment.

When Mary arrived, Arabella made a big fuss and kissed her on both cheeks as she had seen her mother do to her special friends. Mary went bright red while the other children did their best not to laugh. They had all been warned by their parents that morning to be on their best behaviour.

The greetings over, Arabella led the group into the drawing room. She lifted a small silver bell from one of the tables and rang it. Immediately Lydia and another maid entered carrying large silver trays laden with drinks and cakes. The children looked very pleased at this promising start to the day and they couldn't wait to tuck in. Unfortunately, Arabella had instructed the maids to serve her friends because she thought it would impress them. Instead it made things difficult. Most of the children found it hard to choose which cake they wanted, so everything took ages. Before long, some had finished while others hadn't even been served. The children were also worried about spilling something or dropping crumbs. Had they eaten in the kitchen or outside it would have been different, but in the elegant drawing room full of expensive furniture, they couldn't relax at all. What should have been a happy time and full of laughter was really rather awkward, with the children sitting stiff and ill at ease on their chairs. Arabella didn't notice how uncomfortable they all looked, she was far too busy behaving in what she thought was a grown-up way. This actually made her look extremely silly. She kept waving her hands about and laughing too loudly.

Her parents came in to say a brief hello but didn't stay long. They told the children they had things to do. This was perfectly true, but it was also true that they didn't have a clue what to say. They stood for a few minutes smiling awkwardly round at all the boys and girls who sat smiling back, which isn't easy when you have a mouth full of cake and drink. Then they left breathing a sigh of relief that the ordeal was over. It was now time for Arabella's classmates to be taken on a guided tour of the house and grounds, the same tour Mary and Fred had on their first visit.

This was a great success and the children were amazed at what they saw. How could one family have so much? Arabella in turn smiled smugly, everything was going according to plan. Most of the boys were impressed by the video room and wished they had a set-up half as good, while many of the girls fell in love with Pixie and tried to imagine owning such a lovely pony. They all loved the pool and couldn't wait for the time when they could swim.

As the tour went on the children became more and more excited by what they saw and their comments got louder and louder. It became like a competition to see who could do the biggest gasp as they were taken from one luxurious feature to another. Arabella became a little uncomfortable; things were getting slightly out of hand.

At one point her father had to come out of his study to ask them not to be so noisy as he was trying to work. By this time, the children had completely overcome their early shyness and they all shouted 'Sorry!' at the tops of their voices. Arabella's father looked startled and retreated back into his room.

When the grand tour was over Arabella announced that lunch was next, followed by a film in the video room. Then they could swim.

The barbecue started in an organised fashion. But Arabella was not prepared for what happened next. The problem was simply that the children had become hopelessly overexcited. The stress of being in such unfamiliar, rich surroundings, plus the nagging each one had received that morning from their parents to behave, served to create the atmosphere of a pressure cooker. Something had to give and give it did, it was just unfortunate that the pool was so near.

It happened when Carl, the naughty boy of the class, unable to contain himself any longer pushed a hamburger full of ketchup into another boy's face. Carl guffawed with laughter until the boy retaliated by pushing him into the pool, complete with hamburger. Another boy then pushed a girl he had never liked into the water. She went in screaming, with a hamburger still in her hand. This seemed to be the signal for mayhem to break out. Children began pushing each other into the pool while some didn't wait to be pushed and just jumped in.

One boy, who had been lying peacefully on a lounger eating a chicken drumstick, was tipped in but hung on with his free hand, so the lounger went with him. The butler made a wild grab for a girl who had been shoved towards the pool by two others and smiled as he saved her from a watery fate. Sadly, he then lost his balance and the smile disappeared as he teetered on the edge of the swimming pool on one leg, doing a convincing impression of a windmill. If there had been a big splash competition that day, the butler would have won it. He surfaced, blowing a bigger spray of water than any humpback whale ever did. Looking very shocked he began to climb out but was knocked backwards into a half-somersault by a girl hurtling towards him like a missile, into the water.

The screams and giggles were deafening and the whole place seemed full of wet hysterical children with the staff running around madly trying to calm things down. Arabella's father hearing the noise from his study came outside. He looked in utter disbelief at what was going on and then shouted angrily at the top of his voice. There was such bedlam that no one heard except Arabella who, for the first time in her life, felt terribly frightened. Everything was horribly out of control.

Her father realised sterner measures were needed. He marched back into the house, to his desk and from one of the drawers took an old police whistle that he kept there. Back outside he took a deep breath, put the whistle to his lips and blew one long hard blast. He kept blowing until every child was quiet. It took a few seconds, but gradually the splashing and shrieking stopped as everyone looked round to see where the sound was coming from.

Eventually, Arabella's father ran out of breath and the whistling stopped. A silence hung over the pool area as the children began to realise what they had done. They were frightened now, by the madness that had overtaken them, and of Arabella's father, but none looked as frightened as Arabella herself. Her father cleared his throat and said in a dangerously quiet voice. 'The day is now over. Will you please collect your things and go!' Some of the children began to cry, nearly all looked ashamed, while one or two giggled nervously but soon they were all gone as staff took them in doors to dry off, collect their bags and be taken home. The butler clambered out of the pool and staggered away, helped by the gardener. The rest of the staff stood around wondering what to do.

Arabella went to follow her friends indoors, but was stopped short by a sharp blast on the whistle. Fearfully she turned round. Her father's face was twisted with rage and he glared at her with such venom that she found she couldn't meet his eyes and was forced to look away. There came another blast on the whistle. This time her father was standing pointing silently at the pool which was full of bits of bread and sausage and turning pink with ketchup. The lounger floated lazily near the bottom. Then in a cold, hard voice he said, 'Arabella, you are a great disappointment to me. Now get out of my sight.' To the remaining staff he spoke more quietly. 'Perhaps you would clear up this mess, there will be a bonus in your pay packet.' Then he went indoors, back to his study.

'Should have got the little monster to do it,' muttered Cook, 'it'll take ages to clear this lot up.' The rest of the staff agreed and they all turned and stared at Arabella, glad to have a chance to get their own back on the child who had so often made their lives difficult.

In all her life, Arabella had never received such treatment. She stood for a moment staring back at them defiantly, trying to find the words to make a dignified exit, then suddenly she was just a nine year old girl, frightened and terribly unhappy. Her face crumpled, tears started to her eyes and with a stifled sob, she rushed out of the pool area.

The staff watched her go feeling uncomfortable. They didn't like her much but she had looked very distressed and deep down they all felt a little bit sorry for her.

'I blame the parents, muttered Cook and everyone nodded wisely before turning to the task of clearing up.

Chapter 6

Arabella ran to the summer house and flung herself on to the floor. This time her abandoned sobbing was real. All her plans had gone wrong, the wonderful idea had failed. Her father hated her, she could never face the staff again and then there were the children at school on Monday. She could just see them laughing and pointing. Oh how could she bear it? Arabella collapsed in a fit of fresh sobbing and for the next few minutes wept more tears than she knew was possible. She was so sunk in her misery that she didn't notice someone creep into the summer house and sit down on the floor beside her.

Nobody can cry forever, no matter how upset they may be, and gradually Arabella's weeping subsided and hers sobs grew less until they became soft hiccups. She lay where she was, tired and miserable. It was then she became aware of someone beside her. She could feel their hand resting gently on her back. She looked up and there was Mary. 'Oh, it's you,' said Arabella. 'Go away,' she pleaded, 'I don't want you seeing me like this.' A few more tears squeezed themselves out.

'Why not?' said Mary. 'I'm your friend, aren't I?'

Arabella looked hard at her. 'Don't know, are you?'

'I'm here with you now. If I wasn't your friend, I would have gone home like all the others.'

Arabella thought about this, then without warning,

her face screwed up and she began to cry again, softly this time. 'Oh, what am I going to do?'

This was a very different girl to the Honourable Arabella Fitzgerald and Mary wasn't sure what to say.

'Father hates me,' she continued sorrowfully.

'I'm sure he doesn't,' said Mary.

'You didn't see his face.'

'Oh yes I did. He looked very angry.'

'There you are then,' said Arabella.

'All parents get cross with their children sometimes.'

'Mine never have,' observed Arabella.

Mary looked amazed, 'What never?'

'Not like today. It has never felt like this, like he really meant it.' She looked despairingly at Mary. 'Have your parents ever been very angry with you.'

'Oh yes,' Mary replied.

'What, angry like my father is with me now?'

Mary nodded.

'What happened?' Arabella sounded truly interested in spite of herself, so Mary told her.

'Fred and I have always been told never to touch the fire in our front room. It's an open fire and Mum and Dad said we were never to move the fireguard. But one day we did. I got the poker and Fred got the coal shovel and we poked at it like we've seen Mum and Dad do.'

'What happened?'

'There was a big cracking sound and a small coal jumped out and set fire to the rug.' Mary looked frightened even at the memory. 'The rug was old and very fluffy and it burst into flames. Fred and I screamed

51

and Dad dashed in; he saw the fire, then ran to the kitchen and brought a bucket of water and threw it on the flames. It was awful.'

'What happened?' said Arabella for the third time.

'Daddy went wild, he stormed round the room for ages shouting and yelling. Then suddenly he dropped down on his knees beside us and hugged us both really tight. There were tears in his eyes, I've never forgotten that, he was only angry 'cos he loved us and had been very frightened at what might have happened. That night in bed he and Mum came up and when we said our prayers they thanked the Lord for keeping us safe.'

After this long speech, Mary sat looking at Arabella. 'Next day, Fred and I said sorry to Dad and he smiled and said we were forgiven and everything was alright again.'

'Oh,' breathed Arabella, 'setting fire to a rug is almost as bad as what happened today.'

'Worse, I should think,' said Mary heartily. 'Why don't you go and say sorry to your father?'

Arabella looked aghast, then in a voice that reminded Mary of the Honourable Arabella she said. 'I have never said sorry to anyone in my life.'

'Maybe you should - if you are. It would make your father happy. It would make Jesus happy too.' This last comment was made very quietly.

'What did you say?'

'Oh, nothing,' said Mary going red in the face.

'Yes, you did, you said something about Jesus.'

'Well,' responded Mary carefully, as if she were

looking for the right words. 'Dad is always saying it's important to do what the Bible teaches, and in the Bible Jesus says we are to be humble and gentle like him.'

'What's the Bible got to do with anything?'

'It's to do with everything,' said Mary. 'In our house we try to live by the Bible.' Mary remembered her father saying that once.

'Well, it sounds stupid to me,' commented Arabella, uncertainly.

'Oh it's not! It's wonderful!' Mary was so enthusiastic Arabella was taken aback. 'Knowing Jesus and living by the Bible is the best.'

Arabella was confused. She wanted to know what to do about her troubles and here was Mary going on about Jesus.

'What's all this got to do with me?' she wailed.

'Jesus can make it all right, that's what,' said Mary with growing confidence. 'When things seem to go wrong, it's sometimes because God has allowed it so that we can get to know him and trust him better. Maybe he has allowed all this so that I can tell you about him and you will trust him too.'

This was a bit too much for Arabella, but Mary was in full flow so she didn't need to say anything.

'I know what. We'll pray first and then you go and say sorry and I'm sure we will see that God has it all under his control. Shall we do that?'

'No,' said Arabella.

'Oh!' Mary went down like a burst balloon. 'Why not?'

'Because it sounds weird. I don't like what you're

saying. I've never heard anyone talk about Jesus as if he were real.'

'But he is!'

'How do you know he is?'

''Cos, 'cos, 'cos...' Mary stuttered looking for the right words. ''COS HE IS, THAT'S WHY!'

Arabella looked shaken. Mary's outburst had taken her by surprise, but the words had their affect because she didn't argue any more. Arabella didn't know what to think but she knew she had never heard anyone sound more certain about anything than Mary did just then.

'Do you think...' Arabella stopped, she found the name hard to say, it sounded so strange. 'Do you think... Jesus really can help me?'

'I know he can.'

'Are you sure?'

'Yes.'

'Are you really cross-your-heart-and-hope-to-die-sure?'

'Yes,' Mary nodded so hard her head looked as if it might fall off.

'All right then, go on.'

'Go on what?'

'Go on then, pray.'

Mary beamed. 'Okay.'

Now it came to it, Mary felt a little shy but she closed her eyes and bowed her head. Arabella watching did the same.

'Please Jesus, you know all about what has happened today. Please help Arabella say sorry to her Dad and

54

make everything all right. In Jesus name, Amen.'

'Amen,' echoed Arabella. She looked around her as if she expected to see something. 'Is that it?'

'Yes,' said Mary. 'Now go and find your father. I'll wait here and you can come back and tell me what happened.' Arabella hesitated. 'Go on,' said Mary encouragingly. 'Have faith.'

Without being at all sure what 'having faith' meant Arabella got up and walked from the summer house. She took out her hanky and wiped her eyes and blew her nose then looked back at Mary who smiled encouragement.

Feeling very nervous, Arabella made her way to her father's study. Normally she just barged in, but today somehow, it seemed right to knock.

'Come in,' called her father. Arabella took a deep breath, turned the doorknob and entered.

Chapter 7

Arabella's father was busy. Bent over piles of books full of figures he had a frown on his face, the frown deepened when he heard the knock on the study door. 'Come in,' he called shortly. He didn't look up for a few seconds and when he did, was not at all pleased to see it was Arabella. He realised, with some surprise, that she had actually knocked but then he remembered the barbecue and his face became hard.

'Well?'

'Daddy,' Arabella steeled herself, 'I've come to say sorry.' There was a short silence. She looked at her father, willing him to forgive her.

'Have you?' he said. She nodded meekly. 'Well. I should think so. Never in all my days have I seen such goings on.' Her father's voice cracked as all the pent-up anger in him exploded. 'Arabella, your mother and I have done everything we can for you, we have given you everything money could buy. We brought you up to be a lady, to mix with the best people and you let us down by inviting that rabble to destroy our beautiful home. You are not the person I thought you were and I am most disappointed. Now, I am extremely busy.' He returned to his books.

Arabella stared at her father in utter disbelief. She had thought he would give her a kiss her and say, 'That's all right, Snookums.' Instead he was still angry. He really did hate her. Arabella's face went deathly white and her legs felt strange and wobbly. She stood looking at him but as he continued to ignore her she turned and quietly left the room. Closing the door behind her she leant back against it as if seeking strength. Finally, having nowhere else to go she stumbled back towards the summer house.

What Arabella didn't see, was her father after she left the study. A look of great sadness came over his face and his shoulders slumped despondently, like a man carrying a heavy burden. He looked with troubled eyes at the door Arabella had just gone through and then put his head in his hands with a deep groan.

Back in the summer house Mary was all a quiver with anticipation. She saw Arabella coming towards her.

'How did it go?' she called. Arabella shook her head and sat down heavily on the bench seat that ran round the inside of the summer house.

'It's no good, it didn't work.' Arabella looked up at her friend with wide unhappy eyes. Mary was horrified.

'Oh, Arabella, I'm sorry, but I'm sure everything WILL be all right. The Bible says...'

'Mary, I don't care. I don't want to hear any more about the Bible. If your God is there then he either didn't hear or he's not bothered about me.'

Arabella sounded very tired. She desperately wanted to become the Honourable Arabella again who said what she wanted and did what she wanted and didn't care, but she couldn't manage it. Anyway she found she did care, more than she could say.

This sad scene would have gone on for a long tine if someone hadn't called Arabella's name. She knew the voice very well indeed but somehow it sounded different. She looked up and there in the doorway of the summer house stood her father. Arabella couldn't quite believe it and didn't move but just sat looking at him.

He returned her gaze steadily and to Mary it would have seemed, if the idea wasn't so foolish, that they were seeing each other for the first time. Gradually a little smile began in her father's eyes and slowly travelled to the rest of his face. It was a soft, gentle smile just for Arabella; she had never seen him smile like that before. He opened his arms and offered them to her. She hesitated, not sure what to do. He opened them even wider and his smile became broad and welcoming. Arabella didn't wait any longer and ran to him. They hugged each other tight while Mary stood to one side, thrilled beyond words with the way things had turned out.

'I'm sorry, darling,' said Arabella's father. 'I'm sorry I was so hard on you and I'm sorry I got so cross about the silly business with your friends too. I've had a lot on my mind lately.'

It was the first time her father had ever spoken to her in that way and she felt awkward and a bit embarrassed, but also found she quite liked the feeling. She smiled up at her father shyly. Mary noticed this was a very different girl to the Honourable Arabella Fitzgerald. She thought she liked the look of this girl much more, if only she had come to stay.

'I am sorry about everything, Dadsy.'

'I know, but there was no real damage done, just a lot of mess. I expect that will all be cleaned up by now. Except the water of course, that will have to be changed. I don't fancy swimming in ketchup, do you?' Arabella and Mary chuckled. Arabella's father noticed Mary for the first time.

'Still here?' Mary felt very awkward.

'I'm sorry, Mr Brown. I'll go now.

'No need. Stay with Arabella if you want to. I expect there are some burgers left if you go and see Cook.'

Mary smiled warmly at him. He gave Arabella another big hug. 'All right now?' Arabella nodded. 'Good. I'll see you later.' He walked away back to the house. Arabella watched him go then turned and smiled sheepishly at Mary.

'It worked after all.'

'Yes,' said Mary, deeply satisfied with the way things had worked out. 'God always does seem to make things right, but they don't always happen the way we think they should.'

'You're right there,' said Arabella with feeling. The two girls smiled at each other. They both knew something very special had happened and they also knew there was no need to try to find words to explain it.

Chapter 8

Arabella woke on Sunday morning, feeling relaxed and peaceful after a good night's sleep. She stretched lazily then snuggled back down in to the cosiness. The mattress and quilt formed a soft cocoon around her and she was just beginning to doze off when she heard a gentle tap on the door. At first Arabella was irritated, didn't they know she always slept in on a Sunday? Then she remembered. 'Of course,' she whispered to herself, then called, 'Come in.'

A maid entered carrying morning tea on a small silver tray. 'Good morning Miss, it's eight thirty.' Placing the tray on a cupboard near Arabella's bed, she went to open the curtains. The room hardly brightened at all and Arabella realised the day must be cloudy and grey. She watched as the maid returned to the tray and poured out a steaming cup of tea which she placed on Arabella's bedside table. 'Thank-you,' she murmured. The maid looked a little surprised.

'Is there anything else Miss?'

'No, thank-you,' Arabella replied. This time the maid looked pleased. She smiled and nodded before leaving the room to go back downstairs and tell Cook that 'Miss' seemed in a good mood this morning.

Arabella sat up slowly. She shook her pillows, fluffed them, then smoothed the surface. Picking up her tea she lay back against their plump softness. Lifting the cup she took her first sip then let herself slide down a little lower in the bed. Her thoughts turned to the day before.

So much had happened, so much had changed. How could just twenty four hours make such a difference? Arabella knew they could and she had the notion that much of the difference was in her. The idea didn't trouble her, but instead made her feel quiet and comfortable. She found she liked the feeling. It was also hard to believe, but she had agreed to go to church with Mary that day. This was why she had asked to be woken so early and strangest of all, she was actually looking forward to going.

When Mary asked her the day before, at first Arabella said no. She had only ever been to church with her parents at the big cathedral in the city and found the service long and boring; so had her parents judging from their conversation on the way home. Mary assured Arabella that her church was far from boring and that the children did many exciting things, so in the end Arabella said yes. Mary then invited her to lunch and tea, 'we can play all afternoon in my garden for a change,' she'd said.

They went together to ask Arabella's mother who looked doubtfully at Mary. The child was obviously not rich or important, did she really want to encourage their friendship? A phone call to Mary's home changed all that, 'Why didn't you tell me your father is the vicar?' challenged Arabella's mother. For her daughter to play with a village child was one thing, but to spend the day at the vicarage was quite another. It was a most respectable thing to do. Mary's mother was evidently delighted to have Arabella spend the day, so it was all settled there and then. Arabella was also amazed to find out Mary's father was the local vicar, 'No wonder you know all about Jesus and the Bible,' she said.

Arabella put the now empty tea cup on the bedside table. She got up and showered slowly, not wanting to disturb the new quiet way she was feeling. Then she dressed, brushed her hair and made her way down to breakfast. She ate alone as both parents slept in on a Sunday, but found munching hot buttered toast and honey, with just her own thoughts for company, very pleasant. At ten past ten she went out into the hall to find her jacket and to pick up a large oblong gift-wrapped parcel. A maid arrived to tell her the car was ready.

Arabella walked out into a drizzly morning and looked up at the grey overcast sky. It didn't look as if they would be playing in Mary's garden after all. She wondered what they would do instead. Hargreaves opened the passenger door for her and she climbed in with a quiet thank-you. At this, his eyebrows shot up almost to his hairline, thank-yous from this young lady were rare. The look of surprise on Hargreaves face stayed all the way down the drive.

They arrived at the church at twenty past ten and by then rain had begun to fall in earnest. People were scurrying from all directions, some with umbrellas, some with hoods, all glad to dive through the church doors out of the rain.

An enormous golfing umbrella with two legs was waiting outside and as the Bentley pulled up it ran towards them. An arm appeared from underneath the umbrella and started waving madly: it was Mary. Arabella laughed and waved back. Without waiting for Hargreaves to open the door she jumped out and ran to join her.

'I will come to the vicarage at six thirty to collect you, Miss,' called Hargreaves from the driver's seat.

'That will be fine, thank-you.'

Hargreaves' eyebrows almost disappeared up under his fringe. 'Twice in one day!' he thought. He tipped his cap to Mary who called a cheery 'Hello!' then he drove off smiling.

'I'll take you to meet Mum,' said Mary. 'Dad is in his office getting ready for the service, you can meet him later.'

Mary led Arabella into church and the first person she saw was Mrs Carlton. The Headteacher was standing to one side, peeling off a dripping mackintosh. She looked up and noticing the two girls waved at them. Arabella smiled cautiously, while Mary said 'Good morning, Mrs Carlton.'

'Good morning, Mary. How are you today?'

'Wet!' She waved her dripping umbrella and Mrs Carlton laughed. Arabella was taken aback at how friendly the two of them seemed towards each other.

'That's Mrs Carlton,' she whispered.

'I know that,' said Mary.

'But she's the Headteacher.'

'Yes,' said Mary patiently.

'Doesn't she mind you talking to her like that?'

'Like what?'

'Like she's your friend.'

'She is my friend.'

'Oh!' said Arabella surprised.

Mary took Arabella to where her mother was sitting and introduced them. Her mother smiled a lovely big smile and shook Arabella's hand.

'These are for you,' Arabella said, handing her the gift wrapped parcel, 'for letting me come today.' Mary's mother was surprised and delighted.

'Thank-you, Arabella, that is very kind of you.'

Mary took Arabella's arm and led her off to the other side of the church. She had noticed Lydia and wanted to say hello.

Her mother opened the parcel, and what she saw made her gasp. It was a box of chocolates but not the kind you would buy from a supermarket or local sweet shop. Hand-sculptured and imported from Belgium, with exquisite centres. She looked across at Arabella and realised that everything she'd heard about Mary's new friend must be true.

By now, Arabella and Mary were sitting with a crowd of other children of all ages. Some of them had been at the disastrous visit the day before and they carefully avoided meeting Arabella's eyes. She, in turn, felt most embarrassed and didn't look at them.

The service began with Mary's father welcoming everybody and Arabella noticed that he had the same sort of smile as Mary's mother. Then he made a joke about the weather and everybody laughed. No one had laughed in the cathedral and Arabella was surprised; these people actually seemed happy to be in church. Next, after a short prayer, they sang a hymn. It was all about a green hill outside a city and someone who died there. It made Arabella feel sad without her knowing exactly why, but for all that she enjoyed singing it. Then Mary's father gave the children a special talk, just for them and read something very slowly from the Bible.

After that the whole church sang songs about Jesus. The words were cleverly put up on the wall by a special machine. Some of the songs were slow like the hymn, but many were bright and cheerful and had actions. Arabella didn't join in but thought maybe she would next time. All too soon it was time for the children to go out to their own groups.

Mary and Arabella, along with nine other boys and girls, all roughly the same age, trooped into a small room. There were armchairs all round the walls and the children flopped down on to them and began talking noisily. Four of the children had been to Arabella's the day before and it made things a little awkward, but Mary chattered away as if nothing was wrong. Five minutes later a young man, who Mary said was called Don, came dashing in with a pile of books under his arm. 'Sorry I'm late,' he called cheerily and collapsed into an armchair. 'Good morning everyone.' He looked round and noticed Arabella 'and hello to you.'

'Hello,' she responded.

'This is my friend, Arabella,' said Mary joining in. 'She's here for the first time.'

'And jolly nice it is to see you as well,' said Don with a big smile, and some of the children giggled. Arabella smiled back, she liked this young man with his bright breezy ways. Don continued, 'Some weeks I teach this group and other weeks a young lady called Rachel will be here. A particularly lovely young lady she is too.' All the children laughed. Arabella looked puzzled.

'They're engaged,' explained Mary.

'That's right,' said Don. 'She is also a very wise young lady because she said yes to me.' He looked round at the children. 'Now, has anyone got anything to tell us? Anything interesting happen to any of you this week?'

Some of the children looked at each other awkwardly, then at Arabella, then back at each other again. Arabella looked down unhappily. Don noticed but said nothing. 'Come on, someone must have something to tell.'

The next few minutes were spent chatting about the past week and Arabella was glad no one said anything about the day before. When they were finished Don prayed a short prayer and asked God to help them as they learned more about him. Then he opened his Bible and began to read aloud.

Before long Arabella found herself becoming uncomfortable and the other children found themselves watching her to see how she would react. The reading was all about a very rich young man who came to Jesus and asked what he had to do to become one of his followers. Jesus told him to go and sell everything he owned. The young man found he just couldn't and went away sad. Jesus said to the other people who were there, *'It is easier for a camel to go through the eye of a needle than for a rich man to enter the kingdom of God.'*

Don read all of this, without having any idea of what it meant to some of the members of his group and as he finished reading he looked up with a smile. The smile soon faded though as Arabella jumped to her feet and in her worst Honourable Arabella voice demanded, 'Who told you I was coming today?'

Then she turned to the other children with tears in her eyes and shouted. 'I know you all hate me, I know you do! Well, I don't care! I don't care about any of you! I don't care what you think of me! You're just jealous that's all and I think you are all horrible, I hate you!'

She wanted to run away from them, but she was in a strange church and had nowhere to go. Instead she went to the farthest corner of the room and stood with her back to them, her hands over her face.

The children sat stunned. They all looked at Don wondering what he was going to do next. Mary got up to go to Arabella, but Don signalled she was to wait. He handed out work-sheets and pencils to the children and told them to get on quietly. They were all shocked and very glad to have something to do, so they bent over their work without a word.

Don made sure everyone was busy before he went to Arabella and he motioned to Mary to go with him. He realised he would have to be careful, Arabella was a new girl and something was obviously very wrong; he wished it was Rachel's turn to take the class. He pulled a chair over to where Arabella was and sat down beside her waiting as if he had all the time in the world. Eventually he said, 'What is it, Arabella?' She didn't answer. 'Come on, you'll feel better if you talk about it.'

'They hate me,' she said simply.

'Why would they do that?'

''Cos they do.'

'But why?' Don was most puzzled.

''Cos I'm rich and they're not.'

'Oh,' he said, beginning to understand, 'did the reading upset you?'

'You don't have to pretend,' said Arabella haughtily. Don was lost again.

'What do you mean?'

'You knew I was coming today; they told you.' Now Don understood.

'And you thought I chose that reading specially because you were coming?' Don sounded so horrified that Arabella felt less sure of herself.

'I thought they had told you to and you did it without knowing why.'

'Why would they do that?' Arabella hesitated so Don waited patiently. Finally the whole story poured out.

Arabella told him all about being rich and about the disastrous Saturday, how Mary prayed and everything came right with her father. Then she told him how she had woken up that morning feeling nice, nicer than ever before, that is, until he read from the Bible. Arabella was sure one of the children had told him to read that bit just to make her feel awful. Don smiled gently.

'You've had a tough time haven't you?' The way he said this made Arabella feel that he really understood. Then quite suddenly he said. 'It must be nice to be rich.'

Arabella looked surprised but nodded. 'It must be tough too.' Arabella shrugged, she had never thought about it before.

'It brings a lot of responsibilities,' he added. Into Arabella's mind came the picture of her father sitting over piles of books full of figures. This was something he'd always done but she realised with a jolt that just lately he had been spending even more time doing it and that there often seemed to be a worried look on his face too.

Arabella had always thought being rich was easy and something to be proud of. She never thought that it might bring responsibilities. Don continued.

'The reading from the Bible teaches us that God wants us to love him more than the things we own and shows us that following him is more important than being rich.' Arabella was listening. 'It is hard, but being a Christian is not always easy and Jesus wants us to understand that. Once we do understand it and have decided to follow him anyway, then we discover the blessings and there are lots of them, including the promise that one day we will go to be with him in heaven.'

Arabella took a deep breath, 'So you didn't know I was coming today?'

'No, I didn't, but God did. I think he knew you needed to hear this and understand. I wouldn't be at all surprised if everything that has happened is his way of helping you to listen.' Arabella fell silent thinking about what Don had said. A gentle hubbub came from the main church hall.

Don checked his watch, 'Goodness, is that the time?' he looked at the other children and smiled.

'Thank-you for being so good this morning. I think we have all learnt something, don't you?' The children nodded, glad the difficult time was over. Then he said, 'It is going to be tough on Arabella at school tomorrow. I expect you lot to help her.' The children all nodded and smiled at Arabella. She smiled back at them, a rather watery smile but it made her face look nice and they all liked her more because of it.

'Let's pray before we go home,' Don suggested. He prayed for all the children and mentioned Arabella specially, then paused so that everyone could join in with the Amen. The sound of their voices rang round the room and they all knew it had been heard in heaven.

Chapter 9

After church, Mary and her family, along with Arabella, piled into their old estate car and drove home. By now the rain was steady and persistent. There would definitely be no playing in the garden that afternoon. They had travelled less than a mile from the church when Mary's father signalled left and drove through some wooden gates on to a short gravel drive that led to a rambling tumbledown country house.

'We always walk to church in the nice weather,' said Mary's mother looking up at the sky as she threw open the car door and made a dash for the house. Quickly unlocking the front door, she signalled for the children to follow her. Mary, Fred and Arabella jumped from the car and ran inside. Mary's father put the car away into the garage and then spent some time persuading the ancient and rickety garage doors to close properly. Everyone else had their coats off by the time he arrived. He stood on the mat shaking droplets of rainwater from his hair.

Mary's mother took his coat and hung it up with the others, then said briskly, 'Lunch in an hour. Pop the kettle on please, Mary. Fred lay the table will you?'

'Did you hear about the wooden chicken?' said Mary's father. 'She laid a table.'

'Dad, that's awful,' said Mary while Fred chuckled.

'Come on Freddy, my lad, I'll help you.' Off went Mary's father walking and clucking like a chicken, followed by Fred doing his best to copy.

Arabella didn't know what to think, she had never seen anyone's father behave like that. Mary saw her expression.

'Ignore him, he thinks he's funny.' Arabella noticed she was smiling. The two girls went into the kitchen and Arabella watched Mary putting the kettle on to boil and getting out mugs.

'I've never made tea before,' she commented. 'The servants always do that.'

'What do you do if you want a cup of tea and there aren't any servants around?' asked Mary.

'There always are,' said Arabella.

'Well I think everyone should be able to make a cup of tea and cook too. Even the Queen does that sometimes.'

Arabella looked most surprised at this, while Mary's mother hid a smile. She had just poured a Yorkshire pudding batter into hot fat and popped it in the oven. She turned to put the vegetables that were ready in saucepans on to the hob. 'Mary tells me you have a pony, Arabella?'

'Yes,' said Arabella. 'Her name is Pixie.'

'How lovely! I always wanted a pony of my own when I was a girl and I know Mary would love one too. It's very kind of you to let her ride yours.'

Arabella smiled shyly, only she knew it hadn't been kindness that had allowed Mary to ride Pixie, but now she felt ashamed and didn't want to think about it.

'She can come again, whenever she likes,' Arabella said warmly and found to her surprise and delight that she meant it. Mary's father called through from the dining room, 'What did you think of Don?'

'Oh he's very nice,' said Arabella.

'You'll like Rachel, too, they take it in turns to teach Mary's group and sometimes they do it together. Did you enjoy Sunday School?'

Arabella looked at Mary and went a bit red in the face. Mary smiled encouragement. 'It wasn't what I expected,' said Arabella at last.

'Ah, is that good or bad?' Mary's father put his head round the door and pulled a silly mysterious face.

'Dad, leave her alone,' said Mary, and threw a wet dishcloth at her father, who threw it back. It fell into the sink and created a splash that sent washing-up water cascading everywhere.

'Will you two stop it!' said Mary's mother. Arabella saw she was laughing and not at all cross. Never had she met a family that behaved like this and spoke to each other in such a way.

Lunch was a very happy affair. It began with Mary's father saying grace, then her mother handed round plates of roast beef and Yorkshire pudding. She told everyone to help themselves to the dishes of roast potatoes, cauliflower, peas and carrots that were on the table, a large jug of gravy was handed round too. When they had finished Mary's mother produced a large apple crumble from the oven, all golden brown and just the tiniest bit burnt where the apple had bubbled up from under the crumble and over the edge of the dish. It looked delicious and with a good helping of custard poured on top it *was* delicious. For anyone who didn't like crumble there were choc ices from the freezer. Everyone had crumble except Fred who chose a choc ice.

Arabella enjoyed herself enormously, even finding the courage to join in the conversation. Occasionally she made comments only the Honourable Arabella would make but no one took any notice, so it didn't matter.

After lunch everyone helped with the washing up, even Fred. Arabella wasn't asked to help but she felt she ought to. She quite enjoyed herself drying dishes and stacking them on the kitchen surface. When this was finished Mary's father made another pot of tea and everyone sat around the open fire. It was only a small fire because summer was almost there but the sudden rain and the overcast sky made the house feel chilly so a fire seemed a good idea. It created a cosiness that Arabella had never known. The warmth and happiness of that afternoon stayed with her for a long time.

Mary took some board games from a cupboard while Fred laid out his toy cars on the floor. Mary's father succumbed to the warmth of the fire and a full stomach and was soon dozing, peacefully stretched out on an armchair. Her mother took up some embroidery and swung gently in a rocking chair that creaked softly on each backward swing, while the two girls played snakes and ladders and ludo.

Arabella had just slid down the longest snake on the board when she happened to look across at Mary's mother. She watched her sewing for a few seconds then said. 'A camel could never get through there.' Mary's mother looked up. Arabella pointed to the embroidery needle she was using.

'What makes you say that?' she asked kindly.

'Don read from the Bible and it was all about it being easier for a camel to get through the eye of a needle than for a rich person to get into..., to get into...' she looked at Mary.

'The kingdom of God,' said Mary helpfully.

'That's it, to get into the kingdom of God. What's the kingdom of God and why can't rich people get in?'

Mary's mother thought for a moment. 'The kingdom of God is anywhere that Jesus is and if anyone asks Jesus into their life then the kingdom of God is in them. To do this you have to be prepared to give yourself and all that you have to him. It is hard for anyone to give everything to Jesus and follow him. The more a person has, the harder it is, so for very rich people it could seem impossible.'

'Oh,' said Arabella. She looked a little downcast. 'You see, I'm rich.'

'Yes, I know,' said Mary's mother gently.

'So I'm like the camel.'

'No, you're not, not if you are willing.'

'But the Bible says...'

'The Bible says many things and we mustn't take one little bit of it without looking at the rest.' Arabella was puzzled, so Mary's mother explained.

'The Bible also says things like *"with God ALL things are possible"*, and *"to those who believe in His name He gave the right to become children of God"*.' Arabella suddenly understood.

'So I don't have to be a camel; it is possible.' Mary's mother laughed delightedly.

'That's right. Anyone rich or poor can come to know Jesus. It doesn't matter what you have or don't have. It doesn't matter what you've done or haven't done, Jesus is ready to receive you if you give yourself and all that you have to him. He died on the cross to make that possible and to put all our wrongs right. All we have to do is believe and trust him. It really means giving your whole life to Jesus.'

'What about the rich young man in the Bible who went away sad?' Arabella asked.

'He wouldn't do what Jesus asked him to. He wouldn't sell everything he had, which meant his possessions meant more to him than God. That just isn't good enough.'

'Does that mean that if I wanted to enter the kingdom of God I would have to sell everything? Mumsy and Dadsy wouldn't like that.'

Mary's mother smiled. 'No, not necessarily. Jesus was speaking specially to that young man and God deals with each of us individually. The lesson is the same, though, and that is that we must be prepared to give our all. If you give your life to Jesus and tell him everything you have is his and really mean it, then he will be able to show you if there is something that isn't right or if there is something he wants you to give up.'

Arabella had a sudden thought. 'What if he wanted me to give up Pixie? I don't think I could.'

'Well,' said Mary's mother thinking carefully, 'he doesn't ask us to give things up without a very good reason and then he gives us so much in return that in the end it isn't as hard as it first seemed.'

'What if he did though?' Arabella sounded genuinely concerned.

'Then you could still trust him to do what is best for you and Pixie.'

Arabella sat thinking. She could give Jesus lots of things, maybe even herself, but she didn't know if she could give him her beloved Pixie. She was more important to Arabella than anything. She didn't ask anything else and went back to snakes and ladders.

Seeing the conversation was over Mary's mother returned to her sewing. Arabella handed Mary the dice. 'It's your turn, isn't it?' Mary took them, shook them in her hand and threw them onto the board.

'Oh good, a six!'

'Vroom, vroom,' said Fred pushing cars around the floor. The fire crackled, the rain beat against the window and Mary's father began to snore softly.

Chapter 10

It was breakfast time Monday morning but Arabella didn't feel hungry. Instead there was a fluttering feeling deep in her stomach as if a dozen butterflies were trapped there and it made her feel sick. She wasn't looking forward to walking into school and felt worried about how the other children would be towards her. She remembered Don's prayer and clung to it and the children's resounding 'Amen' which somehow seemed to seal it.

Her mother noticed her lack of appetite and put a concerned hand on her forehead but she felt quite cool.

'Are you all right Arabella? You're not coming down with something are you?' Arabella shrugged her off, irritated at her mother's concern knowing she could never tell her the truth.

At a quarter-to-nine, Hargreaves brought the car round to the front of the house. He held the passenger door open for Arabella. Her mother showed concern by standing at the front door of the house and waving as the Bentley drove away.

Hargreaves went to take the long route as he had each day during the previous week and Arabella said quickly, 'The short way today please,' Hargreaves looked pleased, 'and drop me off a little way from the school will you? I'll walk the rest of the way.'

'Certainly Miss,' he said, with a generous smile.

The rain of yesterday was gone and the sun was trying its best to shine, peeping out from behind big fluffy white clouds. Arabella looked up at the sky and thought of God: could he make everything all right today as Don had prayed? She fervently hoped so.

Hargreaves stopped the car some distance from the school and Arabella got out, 'Have a good day Miss.'

Arabella was surprised, Hargreaves never spoke to her unless he had to. She smiled up at him, a thin little smile. He could see she was nervous and remembered Saturday's barbecue. He hoped the children wouldn't be too hard on her. Arabella walked the last few yards to school and into the playground to find Mary waiting for her with three other girls from Sunday School. They all linked arms, with Arabella in the middle and wandered off around the playground. The four girls chattered happily while Arabella remained silent and the butterflies in her stomach became quite demented. Would anyone say anything?

The whistle blew and the girls lined up, two in front of Arabella and two behind. They meant to carry out Don's suggestion to the full and they stood protectively round her, defying their classmates to say something about the events of Saturday. As it turned out, nearly all the children wanted to forget what had happened. Most had received a severe ticking-off from their parents when the truth came out. They all felt ashamed, unable to explain properly how things had got so out of hand.

During the whole of that day there was only one

comment and that happened during first break. A boy ran by the group Arabella was with and shouted, 'Sausage anyone?', but it didn't make him popular as he hoped it would. Nobody else bothered to say anything and the incident was soon forgotten.

That evening after school Arabella went to Pixie's paddock and saddled her. In the past she nearly always got the gardener's boy to do this and had bullied her father many times about employing a groom. He refused point-blank, saying he couldn't employ a man full-time just to look after one small pony.

Arabella then tried to convince him to take up polo and said a string of polo ponies would need a groom.

Her father replied that he didn't want a string of polo ponies and he didn't want to take up polo.

Arabella asked him why not and said it was a noble sport and only played by the rich and famous.

He went on to say he didn't particularly like horses and could see no pleasure in charging dangerously round a field, on a hulking great animal, in pursuit of a small ball.

Arabella said it was the 'sport of kings' and that he should take an interest. Her father replied that horse racing was the 'sport of kings', not polo, and would she please go away as she was making his head ache.

Arabella, like a stuck record, just went on to say that when they had a groom for the polo ponies he could look after Pixie as well.

Her father went red from the neck up, his lips pursed and he looked ready to explode. Then slowly and clearly as if speaking to someone who didn't understand the language, he told Arabella he didn't want to take up polo, that he had no intention of ever taking up polo, that he did not want a string of polo ponies! He did add that if he paid the gardener's boy a bit extra to look after Pixie, would that do?

Arabella grudgingly agreed, but added that her father had missed out on a whole world of excitement and adventure by turning down the polo set.

Arabella remembered all of this now and realised she felt light years away from those days and from the girl she used to be. In fact, it was less than one week and already she was looking back with a sense of shame at her behaviour as the Honourable Arabella Fitzgerald.

Wearing jeans instead of jodhpurs and pushing a riding hat on to her head, she mounted and rode off around the grounds of the house. She had done this more times than she could remember but today was going to be different.

She rode round to the kitchen and called out, 'Hello! Is anyone there?' Lydia heard and popped her head out of the window.

'What is it, Miss?'

'Could you go and ask my mother if I can ride down to the village. Tell her I'll go through the trees and only on quiet roads.' Lydia went to do this.

Arabella's mother came to the kitchen door herself and made a much bigger fuss than Arabella thought was necessary. She said things like, 'You've never left the grounds before', and 'What if you have an accident?'

Arabella said, 'I've got to start going out sometime; I promise to be very careful.' Her mother hardly heard her and carried on, finding reasons why Arabella shouldn't go.

Arabella suddenly opened her mouth wide and screamed as loudly as she could. Pixie jumped violently, Arabella's mother looked stunned and Lydia put her head out of the window again, to see what was going on.

'Why did you do that?' asked her mother.

'Because you won't listen unless I do!' said Arabella, crossly, and sadly she was right.

'Well, don't do it!' retorted her mother. 'It gives me a headache.'

'Let me go out, then.'

'Oh, all right!' agreed her mother, 'But only for one hour, as this is the first time.'

Arabella nodded. She swung Pixie round and, as time was short, cantered off, straight across the gardens towards the gate in the fence where she first met Mary and Fred. The gardener watched her go. He was not at all amused. Hoof prints on his lawn! He made up his mind to have words with her father.

It took Arabella and Pixie ten minutes to arrive in the village and they rode straight to Mary's house. Fred heard the hooves crunching on the gravel and shouted to let everyone know. The whole family were in and so they all came to see the little grey pony.

'I thought you'd like to meet her,' said Arabella shyly, to Mary's mother.

'I certainly would,' she replied enthusiastically,

patting Pixie's neck and stroking her soft nose. Mary was thrilled to see them and Fred rushed off to find a carrot. Then Mary and Fred both had a ride while Mary's father fetched the camera and took lots of pictures. When he was finished he asked for a turn himself and pretended to climb on Pixie's back. For a moment Arabella looked worried, he was far too heavy.

'Don't mind him,' said Mary's mother giving her husband a shove and everyone laughed. Arabella looked a her watch.

'I should be going home now.' She climbed into the saddle and looked down at Mary. 'See you tomorrow.'

'Yes,' said Mary. 'See you.' The whole family watched her go.

'Ride carefully,' called Mary's mother.

Arabella turned in the saddle and waved. She would have to do this again, it was more fun than always riding round her house, Pixie had obviously enjoyed the outing too.

She reached the edge of the trees and hopped off Pixie to open the gate. Once through she hopped on again and put Pixie into a canter. Back across the lawn she went and the gardener watched her gloomily. He would *definitely* have to have words with her father.

Chapter 11

Arabella had been at the village school two weeks. During this time she gradually began to understand about making friends and working with others and though she often made mistakes everyone was very patient. Her classmates were only too glad to forget about the disastrous Saturday and appeared to be making an effort to accept her.

As for Arabella herself, she found by thinking a little before speaking and simply being pleasant that she became more and more popular. It was generally agreed Mary was a good influence but no one took any credit from Arabella, she really was trying her best. Then during the third week two incidents occurred which were to have an effect on Arabella's popularity. The first happened during a games lesson.

Team games were something Arabella had never thought about before. She'd only ever played tennis and then had only ever been partnered by André the coach. Arabella found the concept of netball interesting but confusing, and Miss Little didn't think to explain the game to her - after all, everyone knows netball!

As it turned out Arabella didn't, so when she was put in a team for her first netball match she really had no idea what to do. For the first few minutes she did nothing but stand in the middle of the court watching the other girls charging around her, then she began to get the hang of things - or so she thought.

Unfortunately she completely missed the point. No one had yet had a chance to shoot, so she didn't even associate the nets at either end of the gym with the game. As for passing, she couldn't make sense of it all. Why, after making so much effort running and jumping to catch the ball, should it then be given to someone else? It also seemed to her eyes, that whenever anyone actually got hold of the ball, they became so frightened by the opposing team that they couldn't wait to throw it away.

As she watched, she became filled with a fierce determination not to be so cowardly. So the very first time the ball bounced near her she grabbed it and hugged it to her tightly, shouting, 'I've got it! I've won!'

Her team members screamed at her to pass the ball on but she defiantly clutched it to her chest and shouted back in her best Honourable Arabella voice, 'No. Why should I? I'm not scared.'

A girl from the opposite team became impatient and tried to take the ball from Arabella but the determined girl hung on like a limpet. A tug-of-war followed, which only ended when Arabella managed to wrestle the ball away by being very rough indeed. Then she lay down on the floor with the netball under her tummy and refused to move. The girl tried to push her off but only succeeded in causing Arabella to seesaw on top of the ball. She then became angry and smacked Arabella's legs making her squeal indignantly. Arabella's team didn't actually understand what she was doing but they couldn't stand by and watch her being walloped, so they all rushed over and bundled on top of the offending girl.

In response, the opposing team with blood-curdling yells, rushed headlong into the fray and launched themselves on top of everyone else. Soon there was a pile of girls all fighting like mad on the gym floor with Arabella at the bottom. Their shrieks and screams were deafening.

Miss Little rushed over, bellowing at the top of her voice, 'Stop it girls, this isn't rugby!' Then she began picking the girls off the pile one by one and shoving them away. Eventually Arabella emerged red-faced and breathless, but with the ball still hugged to her tummy. She looked up at Miss Little with a dazed smile on her face and said, 'I like netball!'

Later, when order had been restored, Miss Little blew her whistle for the game to proceed without Arabella. She took the girl to one side and explained the rules. She promised to find a book on netball which Arabella could take home and read for herself.

Remembering what Mrs Carlton had said in the special meeting, Miss Little was very kind and even apologised to Arabella, for not making sure the girl understood what was expected of her. One good thing came out of it all. The other girls thought Arabella was brilliant and tons of fun. This meant she was invited to everyone's birthday parties, so her life became even more colourful.

It was a couple of days after the netball game and two party invitations later that Arabella properly awoke to the pleasures of friendship. After years of being alone, she discovered the joys of life in the classroom. The give and take of working alongside others and the glow of team spirit completely captivated her and she began to look on her friends and teachers with real affection. Which was why the second incident occurred.

It was no longer Arabella's desire to impress her classmates. She began to wish she could find a way of showing her appreciation of them. An idea came to her in bed one night and Arabella being Arabella, she decided to put it into operation the very next day. It meant getting up early and leaving for school an hour before usual but she didn't mind that. So she set her alarm and went to sleep full of anticipation.

Next morning Arabella was woken by the buzzing of her alarm clock and for a second or two couldn't think why. Usually the maid woke her with morning tea. Then she remembered, of course, the wonderful idea, morning tea wasn't due for an hour and a half yet.

Arabella yawned sleepily. She felt very tired and heavy-eyed and knew if she didn't get up straight away she would doze off again, so she staggered from her bed into the shower. This woke her up double-quick because she turned it to the cold setting by mistake. When she'd got her breath back she enjoyed a warm shower but was too excited to spend long soaping herself.

Downstairs she took the staff completely by surprise, asking for breakfast before Cook was even dressed.

A maid was sent to carry a message to Hargreaves in the staff quarters telling him to have the car ready an hour earlier than usual. He was also informed that they would be stopping at the newsagents on the way to school.

Hargreaves had just got out of the shower himself and was brushing his teeth when the maid arrived. He answered her knock on the door and was not pleased to hear what she said and told her so.

The maid replied frostily that she was only bringing Miss Arabella's instructions.

Hargreaves told the maid they were stupid instructions and called her a silly girl for bothering him.

At this the maid became cross and retorted that stupid instructions were appropriate for a stupid chauffeur.

Hargreaves was furious at this cheek and replied haughtily that maids were stupider than chaffeurs.

The maid then declared triumphantly that there was no such word as stupider and even the most stupid maid on the planet knew that.

Hargreaves was trying to think of a suitably clever reply when the maid went on to say not only was he stupid but he looked stupid too, with foam all round his mouth. At that Hargreaves realised he had forgotten to rinse away the toothpaste and was so overcome with embarrassment he slammed the door. The maid laughed all the way back down to the kitchen.

Arabella, blissfully unaware of the trouble she was causing, tucked into bacon and eggs and tea and toast. Cook had prepared this, still wearing her nightie and dressing gown, a large apron tied over the top.

Then Arabella called for the car to be brought to the

front of the house. Hargreaves arrived only just in time and the Bentley's wheels skidded on the gravel drive as he braked a little too hard. Arabella hopped in the back without waiting for him to open the door for her and called a cheery good morning.

Hargreaves just nodded and grunted. He hadn't even had a cup of tea yet, and right at that moment the morning didn't feel too good.

Forty-five minutes later, Arabella walked out of the local newsagents and called happily, 'Send the bill to my father.' After she'd gone the newsagent looked round his shop rubbing his hands together muttering gleefully, 'Might as well go home after the papers have been delivered, there's not much left to sell.'

Hargreaves drove away looking even more fed-up. He had walked backwards and forwards to the Bentley, carrying boxes, more times than he could count. Now the boot and the back seat were full and the whole car low to the ground, weighed down with it's load.

When Mary arrived at school that day, she was surprised to find Arabella already there waiting for her.

'You're early,' she said brightly.

'I had something to do,' replied Arabella mysteriously.

'What?' asked Mary.

'You'll see.'

'Go on, tell me.'

'I'd rather not,' replied Arabella, 'anyway you'll see soon enough.'

Mary felt a little worried, Arabella looked too pleased

with herself. By now other children had gathered round, they too wanted to know what was going on. Arabella wouldn't say anything except, 'You'll soon see.'

For once the children couldn't wait for the school bell to ring and when it did they raced to queue up. The rest of the school looked on enviously, wishing that they, too, were in Arabella's class.

At last the time came and Arabella's classsmates rushed in, jostling excitedly, each one wanting to be first. The teacher in charge called, 'Walk, please', but the children didn't hear and carried on like a herd of stampeding elephants.

When they got to their classroom they all came to a stop in the doorway and the ones at the front gasped in amazement while the others jumped around at the back trying to see for themselves. To their wonder and delight every desk was piled high with packets of sweets, tubes of sweets, boxes of sweets, cartons of sweets and lollipops of every kind. Arabella pushed her way through the stunned children and laughed to see their faces.

'They are all for you, my friends,' she declared joyfully. The children looked at her in disbelief then at each other, no one moved. 'Go on,' she encouraged, 'help yourselves!'

The children needed no second bidding and launched themselves on to the goodies with yelps of delight. Miss Little arrived and stood looking at the goings on as if she were dreaming.

'Class! What on earth...?' The children all looked at

her, their eyes shining with excitement, their pockets bulging and overflowing. Packets of sweets were strewn across the floor. Arabella stepped forward.

'I wanted to do something nice for my friends,' she said warmly, 'and those are for you Miss Little.' She pointed to the teacher's desk and there lay the most enormous box of chocolates. On the lid was a picture of a fluffy white kitten wearing a big pink bow. Miss Little was lost for words, she sat down at the desk looking stunned and bemused. She picked up the chocolates and stared at them.

'Arabella...' she began, but before she could say anymore, Mrs Carlton appeared in the doorway. Under her arm was an even bigger box of chocolates, with an even fluffier kitten on the front, wearing an even bigger pink bow.

'These were on my desk.' Her voice had the same dream like quality as Miss Little's. 'What's going on?'

'It's Arabella,' said Miss Little and both teacher and Headteacher looked at the beaming girl.

'They are for you,' she said warmly, 'because you are my friends.' Mrs Carlton looked at her as if she was seeing her for the first time and the Headteacher's face became soft and gentle, while her eyes looked the tiniest bit moist.

'Oh Arabella,' she said softly. Then she turned to Miss Little. 'Will you call registration then send Arabella to my office please, I think we'd better have a chat.' She smiled encouragingly at Arabella, then left the classroom.

A few minutes later there was a knock on Mrs Carlton's door. She had just finished speaking to Arabella's father on the phone. Once he had calmed down he could see that Arabella meant well and was happy to leave the situation in Mrs Carlton's hands. In the meantime, he said he would telephone the newsagents about taking the sweets back.

Mrs Carlton didn't call 'Come in', as she usually did but went to the door herself and shepherded Arabella into her office. She didn't go to sit behind her desk either, but led Arabella to two cosy armchairs in the corner and together they sat down. Then they had a chat and with Mrs Carlton's encouragement Arabella did her best to explain why she did what she did and how she felt. By the end, Mrs Carlton had reached for her hanky and blown her nose three times, she was so touched by the girl's sincerity. Then she explained carefully and kindly to Arabella that friendship didn't mean someone had to buy expensive presents. True friendship demanded loyalty, kindness and yes, generosity but not quite in the way Arabella had displayed. In reply, Arabella put her head on one side and said in a puzzled voice, 'But isn't it nice to give your friends presents?'

Mrs Carlton replied, 'Oh yes, but not when they are bought with someone else's money.'

Arabella still looked puzzled so Mrs Carlton continued asking, 'Who paid for the sweets?'

'Dadsy,' replied the girl.

'Exactly,' said Mrs Carlton. 'It was your father's money and you didn't even ask him first.'

Arabella looked down and thought about this for a few seconds and she slowly began to see what the Headteacher meant. Her face went a little red and she felt awkward. Suddenly, Arabella turned her gaze on Mrs Carlton, her eyes earnest and imploring. 'What can I do?' The expression on her face was so serious that Mrs Carlton found herself reaching for her hanky again.

A few minutes later, a much happier Arabella returned to her classroom. By lunchtime the boxes of chocolates had been returned to the newsagents. He wasn't very pleased about this, until Arabella's father pointed out that he should never have sold so much to a child in the first place, without her parents being there. So, grudgingly, he took back the chocolates but flatly refused to take back sweets that had been in children's pockets and dropped on the floor. Arabella saw his point and so in the end donated them to the school for use in whatever way Mrs Carlton saw fit.

The Headteacher went to the caretaker's office and collected some black bin liners. Then she went to Arabella's classroom. She asked the children to put all the sweets into the bin liners which they reluctantly did. They all soon cheered up again when Mrs Carlton went round the class telling each child to take two packets each, including Arabella. After this she went round to the rest of the school and gave every other child one packet.

From then on Arabella's reputation grew to giant proportions along with her popularity. This wasn't just with her own classmates but with everyone in the school, even the caretaker developed a soft spot for her.

On top of this her school work began to improve, so as the end of term approached Miss Little felt confidently able to prepare a good report for her newest, most troublesome pupil.

Of course, there were times when Arabella lapsed back into her old ways and say things only the Honourable Arabella would say, but when she did, the other children teased her mercilessly, so they happened less and less.

Chapter 12

After school and at week ends Arabella and Pixie became regular visitors to the vicarage. She noticed more and more how different her life was to Mary's, but she also noticed that Mary didn't seem to mind in the slightest. She asked quite openly why the carpet in the dining room was old and threadbare and Mary answered, just as openly, that her parents were saving up for a new one. Saving was also something Arabella had never considered, she didn't think she liked the sound of it.

Then one day she arrived at the vicarage to find a brand new carpet on the dining-room floor. There in the middle of it sat Mary's mother, proudly patting the soft pile. Arabella had never seen her mother sit on the floor let alone pat the carpet. Mary's mother noticed her expression and said simply, 'It's so beautiful!'

Arabella didn't understand what the fuss was about but recognised that this saving-up seemed to make Mary's family very happy when they finally were able to afford something. She couldn't imagine her parents particularly noticing a new carpet; they had new carpets laid right through the house every three years.

Then there was Pixie. Arabella loved her certainly, but whenever Mary was given the chance to ride she went into such raptures that Arabella thought it a bit strange. She didn't understand the longing there could be in a heart for something as simple as riding a horse, when every ride had to be paid for and there was not much money. Arabella was learning a lot and though much of it did not quite add up yet, all these things were being stored away in her mind.

Having made the break from only riding in the grounds of her home, Arabella discovered the pleasures of exploring the village and the surrounding countryside. Sometimes she went alone and sometimes Mary went with her. On these occasions they took it in turns to ride Pixie or walk side by side holding the reins while the pony meandered along behind them. Other children would sometimes tag along and these outings were often noisy and hilarious, but Arabella liked the times she was alone with Mary the best.

Inside her were many questions about all that she learned week by week at Sunday School. On these walks she would quiz Mary, who did her best to answer.

There was one question, though, that nobody seemed able to give a satisfactory answer to. 'What would happen to Pixie if Arabella gave her life to Jesus?'

She imagined all sorts of things. She even dreamed one night that Pixie died, as God shook his fist from heaven and demanded the best she could give. She awoke, tearful and afraid, and the nightmare stayed with her for many days. Deep down she did think this was wrong.

Don, Rachel, Mary and even Fred, spoke as if Jesus

was a real friend and they insisted a friend wouldn't hurt you, but no one could actually tell her that Jesus wouldn't expect her to give Pixie up. Could she ever trust him enough? She didn't know, yet this gave her no peace and she became more and more aware of a strange sensation deep inside her. It was a hollow feeling, almost as if there was a hole or a gap in her tummy, or was it in her chest? No, that wasn't right, it was deeper inside her, even than that. It made her feel uncomfortable and filled with yearning and a longing for, oh, she didn't know what!

Arabella, in her heart of hearts, guessed that only Jesus was the answer and yet somehow, she was still afraid to trust him completely. In spite of this Arabella was still happier than she had ever been. Her life was interesting and fun and she was learning to like other people and to let other people like her.

This situation could have gone on and on but one day something happened to change it all.

Arabella came down to breakfast on a Tuesday morning to find her father had already left for a meeting. Her mother sat reading the newspaper, a half-empty coffee cup close at hand. Arabella sat down at the table and had just asked the maid for bacon and eggs when her mother closed the newspaper, folded it and put it down in a very determined fashion. It seemed to Arabella almost as if she had just arrived at a decision and she looked at her mother expectantly.

'Arabella,' she said, in a firm voice that sounded as if she knew Arabella wasn't going to like what she was about to say. 'Your father and I have made a decision. We think you have been spending altogether too much time with the children from the village and we are not happy about their influence on you. We have brought you up for higher things and mixing with these people has lowered your standards; you are not the girl you once were.'

Arabella opened her mouth to say something but her mother raised a hand to silence her and continued, 'We have decided that the village school is not the best for you and have arranged for you to start at Lady Worthington's at the beginning of the autumn term.'

She raised her hand again as Arabella started to object. 'It is not open for discussion, this is what is going to happen. I know you will not thank us now, but in the future you will be grateful. Once you have started at Lady Worthington's there will be no need for you to see the vicar's daughter any more. I happen to know that there is a daughter of an Archbishop at your new school who will be far more suitable company for you. As for church, we will be happy to have Hargreaves drive you to the cathedral in the city each Sunday, so there will also be no need for you attend the village church either.

Throughout this speech Arabella gradually took on the appearance of a fish out of water. She stared open-mouthed with horror at her mother and gasped for air. She felt dizzy and sick as her wonderful new world crumbled before her. Her mother was rather taken aback by this reaction. She had carefully rehearsed what she had to say and felt pleased with the way it came out. Now she felt a good deal less confident. She hadn't expected Arabella to look so distressed; surely the child knew they were only doing what was best for her.

For once in her life Arabella could think of nothing to say. Actually that wasn't exactly true, she could think of plenty to say but it all involved screaming and shouting and crying until she was sick. Yet to do that would not adequately express how awful she felt at that moment.

She sat desperately trying to find the words that would explain clearly to her mother how she felt. Her mother took the silence to mean acceptance and this worried her more than she could say. When Arabella screamed the way she used to, everyone understood what was going on. This quiet, serious Arabella was far harder to understand and deal with.

Her mother got up from the breakfast table feeling uncomfortable. Now the grand speech was over, she didn't know what to say to her daughter. She also had the feeling that Arabella's father would not be pleased with her. Why had everything become so complicated? The edge of a headache began to throb and with a hand lifted to the side of her face she left the dining-room.

Arabella sat staring at the table as Lydia bustled in with her breakfast. She put the plate in front of her, before noticing how distressed the girl looked. 'Why, whatever's the matter, Miss?'

Arabella swallowed hard and tried to answer, instead she hiccuped and found that words just wouldn't come.

'Oh Miss, try to tell me, shall I fetch your mother?'

Arabella quickly shook her head and looked up at Lydia pale and wide-eyed. 'Are you feeling ill?'

Arabella shook her head again and breathed deeply until the tightness in her chest grew less and she was able to speak.

'They're taking me away from school, from church, from Mary,' she whispered. She told Lydia what her mother had said.

'Oh Miss.' Lydia wanted to comfort the girl but didn't like to touch her employer's daughter. She, like the rest of the staff, had noticed a change in Arabella. They all agreed it was for the better and Lydia couldn't understand why Arabella's parents couldn't see it too.

Suddenly she blurted out, 'Tell him Miss. Tell him all about it, he can make it right. Sometimes things happen that seem so awful, but if we give them to him he can bring good from them.'

It took Arabella a few seconds to realise that Lydia was speaking of Jesus. She was the second person to say this. Arabella remembered Mary in the summer house - it had worked out all right then, could it happen again? Into her mind came Don's prayer - no, this was the third time she had heard it and found it to be true.

Suddenly, Arabella knew they were right, she couldn't have said how she knew, she just did. With desperate, yet hopeful eyes she looked up at Lydia.

'Would you ask him for me? I don't know how.'

Lydia hesitated, then nodded. She closed her eyes and bowed her head, Arabella did the same.

'Dear Jesus, you know what has happened and the

plans that have been made for Miss to go to a new school and a new church with new friends. You see how sad she is; please, Lord, come and help her. We trust you to work things out for the best. Thank-you that you always hear our prayers. In your name, Amen.'

'Amen,' whispered Arabella and gave Lydia a little smile. 'Thank-you,' she said, 'I feel a bit better now.'

'That's right, Miss, now eat your breakfast and get off to school and try not to worry. God's in charge now.'

Arabella found she could manage to eat a little of the bacon and eggs in front of her. She was sure what Lydia said was right, that God was in charge of the situation.

Then like a lightening bolt Arabella realised that while this might be true, he wasn't in charge of her. She had never given him herself, not yet anyway. Was she ready now to trust him with everything? Immediately into her mind came Pixie.

'I'm sorry,' she whispered. 'I can't. You might take her from me.'

Chapter 13

At school Arabella told Mary and her friends what her mother had said that morning at breakfast. They were all terribly upset and did their best to reassure her, offering words of advice and sympathy.

As the news spread through the class, Miss Little overheard snippets of what the children were saying. When Arabella seemed distracted during lessons and unable to concentrate, she guessed it was probably true.

At the first opportunity she spoke to Mrs Carlton, who looked distinctly concerned and called for Arabella. The Headteacher and pupil had a very helpful chat for almost twenty minutes and Arabella left the office feeling comforted. Mrs Carlton then sat and pondered the best way to tackle things.

That evening Mary went home and told her mother and father. Another girl who was in Arabella's Sunday School group as well as her class at school happened to bump into Rachel in a shop after school and told her too.

Over the next few days Arabella's father received one phone call and two visits. The phone call was from Mrs Carlton who wanted to have a chat with him over something that had come to her ears: would he mind popping into her office to confirm or deny the rumours? He was most puzzled but readily agreed.

The visits were from, first of all, the local vicar. He was concerned about talk that Arabella was to be taken from church and friends. He asked Arabella's father politely if there was any truth in these stories and then expressed concern for the child's welfare as she did seem very happy and settled.

The second visit was from Arabella's Sunday School teachers. They were a young couple who looked very comfortable together; Arabella's father noticed the girl wore an engagement ring. They asked in a very caring, friendly fashion about Arabella and hoped that the rumours they had heard about her being taken away were not true. She really did seem to enjoy their classes and they would miss her very much.

Arabella's father was most surprised by all the concern over his daughter. He told each caller he knew nothing of any changes that would affect Arabella. However, he would try to find out where the rumours were coming from.

After Don and Rachel's visit he called for Arabella, who came to his study. They chatted for a few minutes and Arabella told him all that her mother had said. She ended by saying, 'Daddy, why are you sending me to Lady Worthington's and taking me from my friends?'

In reply her father kissed her on the forehead and told her she was not to worry any more. Then he went off in a very determined fashion to find his wife.

That evening Arabella's family sat down to dinner. The chat with her father had reassured Arabella enough for her to do justice to her food. This was a good thing because Lydia had told Cook about what had happened.

Cook, in turn, wanted to do something to cheer the child up, so she prepared her favourite meal.

Arabella was delighted to find melon cocktail, chicken chasseur and lemon meringue pie with ice-cream on the menu and tucked in.

Later on, she did something she had never done before and went to the kitchens to thank Cook. Cook was so amazed she did something she had never done before and hugged Arabella.

On the other hand, dinner for Arabella's mother seemed to be a strain. She did little more than play with the food pushing it around the plate with her fork in a distracted manner and putting hardly anything in her mouth.

After dinner Arabella's father told the maid that they would have coffee in the lounge. Arabella didn't like coffee and was about to run off and play, when her father said, 'Arabella, will you join us, I have something to say.'

Arabella's mother looked at her unhappily and Arabella felt a cold shiver run down her back. Was this what she had been waiting to hear? Were her parents about to tell her about her future?

Arabella's father took his wife's arm in a strong, comforting way and led her from the dining room. There was something in the way he did this that worried Arabella and made her wonder what on earth she was going to hear. She followed her parents apprehensively.

Once in the lounge, Arabella's father helped his wife

to the sofa, pulled a small footstool up for Arabella to sit on and then dragged an armchair over for himself. It looked to Arabella as if he were trying to make sure they sat as near together as possible - it felt as close to the cosiness of Mary's house as Arabella had ever known.

The maid brought the coffee and Arabella's father said, 'You may leave us now, I will pour. Please make sure we are not disturbed for at least half an hour.'

The maid nodded and said, 'Yes sir.' She left the room and rushed to the kitchen to tell cook.

'Something is going on, I don't know what, but something is.'

'I dare say we will know soon enough, if it is anything to do with us,' said Cook briskly. She put the kettle on to boil and the women sat down, glad to have a break and the chance of a chat.

Back in the lounge, Arabella's father looked at his wife and daughter fondly and smiled at them in a most affectionate way. They looked back at him expectantly and Arabella felt reassured by the kind expression on his face. She looked at her mother who obviously did not feel the same reassurance, for she sat upright and stiff, her fingers clutching nervously at the hem of her dress.

Arabella's father began to speak, the words came out slowly as if he wanted to make quite sure they understood.

'I have some news. Arabella, your mother knows something of what I have to say, but I think the time has come to tell you both, quite clearly, what has happened.'

Arabella looked at her mother - were those tears in her eyes? Surely not, her mother never cried. Her father continued, 'Business has not been good lately and there have been some mistakes made. I'm afraid I've lost a great deal of money and there will have to be some changes in our lifestyle.' He went on to tell them just how bad things were and that he would have to raise a lot of money very quickly or else they would lose everything. There was only one way to raise such an amount and that was by selling the house and most of what they had.

From now on, there would be no more servants and no more swimming-pool. They would have to move into a house in the village, not somewhere horrible, but certainly something fairly ordinary. Life would change completely for them and he wanted his family to know and understand why this had to be. He suddenly looked very sad and old. As Arabella's mother gave into tears, he put out a hand and took hers and offered the other one to Arabella. She took it gladly and then reached out to her mother. The family sat in a little circle thinking their own thoughts about what the future held.

Suddenly Arabella said, 'It won't be so bad, you'll see. Mary and her family are ever so happy and they're not rich. I helped wash up after dinner when I spent the day and it was fun. We can all help wash up, Mummy, everything will be all right.'

Arabella's mother wiped her eyes and looked doubtfully at her daughter, she didn't feel so sure, but her father said as cheerfully as he could, 'That's right. That's the attitude. We'll be all right. Tomorrow I'll take you to see the house I've found and if you like it we will move next month.'

Arabella's mother got up from the armchair and, without a word, left the room. Her father watched his wife go with concerned eyes, but didn't attempt to follow her. Arabella waited until she was sure her mother couldn't hear before asking, 'Daddy, why did Mummy tell me I had to leave my school and go to Lady Worthington's when she knew we weren't rich any more?'

Her father sighed, 'Because she didn't want to believe the bad news I suppose. I think it was her way of fighting back. I'm sorry you were frightened but there's no need to be now. Things will be tough for a while, but I promise you everything will be all right. After all we still have each other, don't we?'

He smiled at her, a tired but kind and loving smile and Arabella realised that while Pixie was no less precious, she certainly wasn't the most important part of her life.

Chapter 14

Arabella needed a place to think. The news had come as a great shock to her, though she'd tried to hide it for her parents' sake. Now she needed somewhere to go and sort out how she felt. She knew the very place.

The warm summer evening wrapped itself around her as she made her way to the east gardens and Arabella sighed at the familiar sights and sounds of her home. Then she remembered, it was not going to be home much longer. The thought made her feel peculiar and she was glad to arrive at the summer house.

She didn't go straight in, but stood looking with her head on one side. She realised the building was like an old friend, someone she could turn to when comfort or help was needed. Then it occurred to her that she hadn't visited her old friend for ages, not since the dreadful Saturday and she wondered why, when she used to spend so much time there. Suddenly she knew and the answer was simple, she had Mary now and many other friends at church and school. A summer house was poor company compared to real people. Yes, her life had certainly changed.

She went into the summer house and sat down on the wooden seat. It was time to think. Relaxing back against the wall Arabella closed her eyes and let her mind drift.

Straight away she remembered Lydia's prayer. Once

again everything had worked out, her life wasn't going to change. This thought was quickly replaced by another; of course her life was going to change and change dramatically. Yet somehow this did not disturb her as much as the earlier fear of losing Mary and her new life. Arabella knew that this was the real issue, this was what she needed to think about. Could it be that her new life mattered more to her than her old? Surely not, that couldn't possibly be. Being rich and having a big house with lots of lovely things and feeling important were what mattered in life. Weren't they? For the first time Arabella wasn't so sure. Could it be that these things were not so important as she once thought?

Into her mind came a series of images. She thought of her father's face and remembered her mother's tears. She thought of Mary and Fred, of Lydia, of Don and Rachel and school. She thought of Mary's parents in the glow of an open fire and of Mrs Carlton calling good morning in church. These were what really mattered to her now. Last came the staggering thought that God had been in control of it all; it was all to help her understand and somehow that mattered most of all.

Arabella sat up as if she had been stung by a bee. New understanding filled her mind, illuminating everything just as floodlights illuminate a darkened stadium. She saw the big house, the swimming pool, the video room and all that she once held dear, only now they seemed pale and shadowy, without any real substance. How could she have ever thought that they could make her truly happy?

Arabella swallowed hard as the picture of a camel, standing beside the impossibly small eye of a needle, came clearly into her mind. She watched fascinated as the eye began to grow and grow and grow until finally, when it was large enough, the camel lowered its head slightly and stepped through. Like an echo she heard the words, 'With God all things are possible', and Arabella knew, as the camel stepped through the eye of the needle, that she stepped through with it straight into the kingdom of God.

'To those who believe in His name He gave the right to become children of God.' Arabella remembered the words. She looked back on the Honourable Arabella Fitzgerald as if from the top of a high mountain and found her small and silly and quite insignificant. She had emerged as a butterfly does from its chrysalis, never to go back to the old life again. She was quite simply a new creature.

There was no longer any doubt inside her; come what may she knew her life was in God's hands. Arabella put her hands on her tummy. The hollow feeling was gone. Now she felt full and whole and complete. The deep longing had been replaced with joy and pleasure. These bubbled together and filled her to such a point that she felt she must burst with happiness.

Jesus was her friend and without learning the words, her very being sang a song of praise.

How long she sat there she didn't know but when the first glory of that glorious moment subsided the sun was almost gone and twilight had come. Reluctantly, she checked her watch. It would soon be time for bed but she was filled with such an energy she wondered how she would ever manage to sleep. She had about fifteen minutes before they would be calling for her to go indoors and there was something she had to do first. If she hurried, there would just be time.

Arabella jumped to her feet and ran from the summer house across the garden. She ran past the swimming pool area and down the path to the paddock. The gardener's boy had already brought Pixie in for the night, so Arabella went straight to the stable. Opening the lower half of the door she bent under the top half and went inside.

Pixie whinnied with pleasure at seeing her mistress. Arabella stroked her lovingly and scratched her behind the ear. The pony bent her head gently towards Arabella and a great surge of affection filled the girl. She knew what she had to do.

Her hands were trembling as she placed one on either side of Pixie's face, then looking up Arabella whispered, 'She's yours now. I know I can trust you with her. I'm sorry it's taken so long.'

She leant forward and laid her face against the pony's. She expected to feel sad as though she had lost something, but instead was filled with a sense of wonder, because what she felt was safe. She and Pixie were now truly safe.

Arabella gave the pony a final pat before leaving the stable. She felt peaceful inside and knew she had done the right thing. Walking back towards the house she heard someone calling her name, telling her it was time to come in and her thoughts turned to the hot chocolate she knew was waiting.

A tiredness suddenly swept over her and with it came a deep longing to curl up in her soft bed and go to sleep. Arabella yawned and for a moment wondered what tomorrow would bring.

Chapter 15

Next day after school, Arabella and her mother and father took the Bentley and drove to the village. Arabella recognised the way they were going - it was the same direction as the vicarage, only her father didn't stop there but drove past. He went a few yards further on, turned left into a leafy avenue and pulled to a stop outside a detached house standing in its own grounds.

Arabella could see that it was a far cry from where she lived now. Her mother looked at it as if she was being asked to move into a garden shed. Arabella thought it was nice and said so; her father looked pleased. He'd collected the key from the estate agents earlier in the day and as the owners had already moved, it meant the family could have a look round on their own, with no one to bother them.

There were four good sized bedrooms, two bathrooms, a lounge, a dining room, a big fully-fitted kitchen, a utility room and a walk-in larder.

Arabella spent a long time looking round, even checking in every cupboard, while her father who had seen the house before, pointed out the features. Her mother glanced briefly in each room before going back downstairs.

'What do you think?' said Arabella's father, trying be cheerful.

'It's all right,' said Arabella in a positive way.

'Is it really?' He looked at his wife. She shrugged and went out to the car. Her father looked disappointed.

'Can I see the garden, Daddy?'

'Of course.' He led Arabella out through the back door into a spacious lawned garden, edged with flower beds and shrubberies.

'It's nice, but I will miss all our land. Where will I ride Pixie? I suppose it will have to be out in the village, what a good thing I've already started getting used to riding on roads. I've been wondering, where are we going to keep her?'

As Arabella chattered gaily on, her father looked more and more uncomfortable. At the last question she turned to him for an answer and saw his face. 'What is it Daddy? What's the matter?'

'Oh, Arabella,' he started, then paused trying to find the right way to say what had to be said. 'I thought you understood, we have to sell *everything*.'

'Yes, I know. The house and the land and the swimming pool and no more servants.' It suddenly dawned on her what he meant. 'That doesn't mean Pixie too, does it?' she said slowly.

Her father's face told it all, Arabella was shocked.

'Oh, Daddy, you don't mean we have to sell Pixie?'

'Arabella, I'm sorry, there just won't be the money to keep a pony.'

'I didn't know you meant Pixie.' Arabella was frantic.

'Surely we can afford her, she's only a little pony. She doesn't eat much. If I promise to eat less and not ask for things can I keep her? Please, Daddy can I keep her?' Arabella's father looked upset and shook his head.

'I don't think so darling, I really don't think so. Look, I will go back and check the figures again. I have a team of accountants coming in to tidy everything up and I will ask them if we can afford to keep her, but I really don't think it is possible.'

Arabella looked so stricken that he wanted to say something to comfort her. He tried to put his arm around her shoulder but she shrugged it off and ran out to the car. She dashed over to her mother.

'He's going to sell Pixie! Tell him he can't, Mumsy, please tell him he can't!'

Her mother got out, and forgetting her own troubles for a minute, put her arms around her daughter. 'I know darling. I know, but what can I do, what can any of us do?'

Arabella's father came slowly towards them, his hands were thrust deep in his pockets and his head was down. Both mother and daughter turned to glare him. It was all his fault!

In that moment, several things flashed into Arabella's mind. She remembered the summer house last evening and the joy of discovering Jesus. She remembered going to the stable and handing Pixie over to God and the peace that followed. She remembered her father's face as he broke the news and she knew, without a shadow of doubt, that it was quite wrong to make him look so sad now.

In her heart she whispered sorry to God and the strangest thing happened, the peace came flooding back. Nothing had changed that she could see, but there was no doubt that she felt different. Suddenly, along with the peace, came hope, a real solid hope that only comes from faith.

'I'm sorry, Daddy.' She ran to him and threw her arms around him.

'Why are you sorry? It's me that should be saying sorry to you.'

'I'm sorry that I was cross about Pixie. If she has to be sold I will try my best not to mind too much.'

Here Arabella's voice broke, making it quite plain how much she would mind, but she did her best to smile up at her father, though it was a rather wobbly smile.

He looked down at her in utter amazement. This was almost a different girl to the one he knew or thought he knew. Arabella's mother was also quietly amazed at her daughter's reaction.

'What's happened to you, Arabella?' said her father curiously.

In spite of herself Arabella wanted to laugh.

'Do you really want to know?'

'Why, what's going on?'

'I'll tell you on the way home.'

So she did and by the time they got back to their house two very bemused and slightly concerned parents went in for dinner.

Later on, when Arabella was in bed, her father made a telephone call to the vicarage. He was worried about

Arabella and wasn't sure he wanted his daughter to get caught up in 'religion'.

Mary's father listened to all he had to say, then said the telephone wasn't the ideal way to talk and could he come round to speak to him and his wife in person? If it would help, his wife could come too.

In the end Arabella's father invited them to dinner the next night. He said, 'As our daughters seem so keen on each other it might be a good thing to become acquainted.'

Mary's father said, thank you very much, they would be delighted to come and he was sure they wouldn't have any problem finding someone to sit on Mary and Fred. This was his way of saying 'baby-sitter', but Arabella's father thought it a very strange way of putting it, especially coming from the Vicar!

Up in her bedroom, Arabella was finding it difficult to sleep. She tried to imagine life without Pixie and couldn't. Then she tried to imagine her family living in the house in the avenue, instead of here where they had always lived; again she couldn't.

How would her mother manage without servants?

What would the servants do without their jobs?

How do people keep cool in the summer if they haven't got a swimming pool?

Arabella's head was in a total whirl, she sat up in bed tired, hot and bothered.

She was about to lie down again, with no hope of sleep, when something Mary said came back to her.

'In our house we try to live by the Bible...' The Bible!

Could that help? She wished she owned one, but of course she didn't. Did her parents? She racked her brains trying to remember ever seeing a Bible in the house, then it came to her. Of course, the family Bible in her father's study.

She could remember, when she was little, being shown her name in the family Bible, it was the last entry in a long line of names. Everyone there was a part of the family tree that reached back down the years to seventeen hundred and something. Arabella got out of bed and crept downstairs. She heard her father on the phone in the drawing room but didn't stop to listen, most of his phone calls were boring.

Arabella tiptoed into the the study, closed the door behind her and put on the light. She went over to the bookshelves and sighed heavily. She hadn't realised quite how many books her father owned. One wall was almost entirely lined with them and she wondered how she would ever find what she was looking for. In fact she found the Bible very quickly simply because it was the biggest book there. It was a huge tome that reminded her of the one she'd seen in the cathedral. If anything this was bigger, and looked so heavy she began to doubt whether she would be able to even move it. At least it was on a low shelf.

Arabella took hold of the back of the book and pulled. It didn't budge. Not only was it big and heavy, it didn't look as if it had been moved for years. As it turned out she was right, it hadn't.

Arabella took a firmer grip, she tugged and tugged.

Suddenly the book gave slightly. She put one foot up on the book case and leant back pulling with all her might. Without warning the enormous Bible slid out in one go on to the floor and Arabella fell flat on her back.

The fall winded her slightly but also made her giggle, she thought how funny she must have looked - wouldn't Mary have loved to see that? She giggled again and as you know one giggle often leads to another and soon she was quite helpless. She kept thinking of herself lying on her back in her father's study having hysterics and that would set her off again. Arabella stuffed her hand over her mouth to stifle the noise. She wasn't afraid of being caught but what she was doing was private and she didn't want to have explain herself.

In the end quite a few minutes were lost before Arabella regained control and sat up, wiping her eyes on her nightie. Then she turned to the Bible and opened it up at the family tree. There were all the names of one side of her family, the first was dated seventeen sixty-four. She ran her finger down the list. The last name was her own, written by her father nine years before.

One day she would be gone and Arabella wondered if in hundreds of years' time, another girl would sit and look at her name too. This last thought was too weird and made Arabella feel creepy. She remembered why she had come. Pushing her hand under a wad of pages, she turned them over. Could God really speak to her from this dull-looking book? Arabella started to read.

It wasn't long before she realised she had a problem. This Bible was nothing like the one Don read from on a

Sunday but had very old-fashioned language. The odd bit she read made little or no sense to her and she shook her head in frustration.

Arabella's mood changed to one of despondency. As soon as she could she would get a Bible like Don's, but tonight it seemed she would have to go back to bed without any words of comfort.

As the Bible was heavy and unused to being opened the bulk of it snapped shut as soon as she began to close it but Arabella had hold of the right hand cover and some pages as well so that part remained open. She was about to close the book completely when something caught her eye. It was only a short sentence and it wasn't underlined, but the words stood out so clearly it might as well have been. *'And we know that all things work together for good to them that love God.'*

She caught her breath, not only could she understand, but this was exactly what she needed to hear. She read it again marvelling at the way the words so suited her situation.

Arabella grabbed another book from the shelf and placed it like a bookmark in the Bible, so the reading wouldn't be lost. She went to her father's desk to find a pen and paper. She carefully wrote the words out, checking to make sure they were copied correctly, then read them again.

Now all she had to do was return the Bible to the shelf. This took a monumental effort as she was beginning to feel very tired, but with a struggle she managed it.

Arabella went back to her room making sure she turned off the light and closed the door to the study.

Before getting into bed she read the verse once again and whispered a heartfelt 'Thank-you!' Then she lay down, and pulled the quilt up under her chin.

Five minutes later she was fast sleep, her mouth curled up into a little smile and her hand clutching the precious paper.

Chapter 16

Over the next few days, Arabella needed that verse from the Bible. She looked at the paper many times and finally memorised the words. They were a great comfort as all the changes to her life got under way.

The dinner party for the four parents was a great success. Mary's father was able to reassure Arabella's parents about her new faith. He told them their daughter was far happier and contented with life knowing Jesus. As Arabella's parents had already seen evidence of this, they couldn't argue. They were curious for themselves too and asked lots of questions which Mary's parents did their best to answer. They all got on so well that Arabella's father felt he could tell them about losing the house, which he did.

Mary's parents were deeply shocked, how terrible for the family. Suddenly, it was all too much for Arabella's mother and she began to weep. Mary's mother went to her and put her arms round her. The two men went out into the garden to leave the women alone and Arabella's mother at last found someone she could really talk to. In the end, Mary's parents didn't get home until nearly midnight. Mary and Arabella were both most surprised to discover their parents were having dinner together. They were extremely pleased too; it would be lovely if they could all become friends.

Arabella told Mary about everything at the first opportunity. This happened one evening after school when Mary came to play and stay for tea. She was speechless with delight at her friend giving her life to Jesus and hugged her.

Then she became speechless with horror as she learnt Arabella was to lose her home. She became speechless with delight again when she discovered Arabella's new house was just around the corner from hers, and was then immediately speechless with horror as she heard Pixie was to be sold. All-in-all, Mary didn't say much.

When Arabella finished telling her, the two girls linked arms and walked together to the summer house where they sat and prayed about everything, especially Pixie. Mary was amazed to find Arabella so peaceful in the face of losing her beloved pet, but as Arabella said, 'She's not mine any more, I gave her to Jesus. He will do what is best.'

Mary, who had grown up knowing nothing else but Christianity, was deeply affected by her friend's new faith. She wondered if she would have been quite so calm, faced with what Arabella was facing.

Arabella was indeed trusting God to bring good out of the situation as the verse in the Bible promised he would. Pixie had been advertised in all the best horsey magazines and so a succession of hopeful buyers duly arrived.

The first was a very chubby girl in tight jodhpurs. Her hair was scraped into pigtails which stuck out either side of her riding hat. Her mother came too, wearing a very fashionable suit with matching shoes. Highly unsuitable for viewing a pony, Arabella thought.

Pixie was saddled and bridled and brought out by the gardener's boy. He held her while the girl scrambled up on to Pixie as if she was climbing a ladder. Then she pulled the pony around with rough hands which caused Pixie to yawn wide as the bit cut into her soft mouth.

Arabella made up her mind this particular girl was *not* getting her hands on her darling pony! When the girl said she wanted to buy Pixie, Arabella gave a long list of the pony's faults which caused the gardener's boy to look very surprised, but put the girl and her mother off.

The second child was a boy. His mother came as well. She was very different to the first girl's mother. This lady came wearing jodhpurs and green Wellingtons. She wore a waxed jacket even though it was a warm day and had a scarf on her head tied under her chin. She shouted at her son to take control of the pony and show her who was boss. The boy looked very determined and thumped his heels into Pixie's side and waved the rein like a charioteer. Pixie didn't understand what was expected of her and stopped. The mother shouted even louder and the boy waved the reins even harder and drummed his heels against the pony's side.

Arabella became very cross and took hold of Pixie's bridle. She told the boy to get off at once and that she wouldn't sell him her pony if he was the last person on earth. At this, both the boy and the mother left disgusted.

After these two, came a succession of people ranging from nice to dreadful. From the quiet mouse of a girl

124

who just sat on Pixie letting her do what she liked, to the very efficient boy rider who was looking for something to use at gymkhanas. From the girl who came with her father, who hunted locally and wanted something for his daughter to start hunting on, to the child who was very nervous and wanted something quiet and friendly.

Arabella got into the habit of dropping Pixie's many faults into the conversation and watched as everyone decided she wasn't the right pony for them. The faults were, of course, made up but Arabella was finding it hard to cope with the idea of anyone buying her beloved Pixie.

In her own mind she had entrusted the pony to God, but was, in fact, doing her level best not to let her go. 'They are all so horrible,' she reasoned, and though this was not absolutely true, it made her feel better.

The moving day drew nearer and even for Arabella's father, who was trying his hardest to look on the bright side, the strain began to tell. It was hard having people look round his lovely home all of them saying how they wanted to knock a wall down here or remove a fireplace there. One couple even spoke of painting the oak panelling in the hallway. Arabella's father bit his tongue and made a mental note that they would not be buying his house.

The team of accountants arrived and spent many days in the study going over piles of figures. They would be the ones to say how much money would be left at the end of the day. Judging by what Arabella's father said they doubted if there would be enough for the family to keep a small grey Welsh Mountain pony.

It wasn't long before Arabella's father began to notice that the steady stream of prospective buyers who made their way down to the paddock all left without wanting Pixie. He became a little suspicious and one day followed a family down to the stables. He kept his distance and then hid within earshot.

He soon found out what was going on as Arabella told the family that Pixie was inclined to kick and could be vicious in the stable. Sometimes she limped due to an old injury and would buck at every opportunity. She got a bit carried away and gaily told them that the pony was thoroughly dangerous, not to be trusted and that she wouldn't let any child of hers get up on her. The family looked doubtfully at this monster of the horse world, while Pixie stood meekly, looking exactly like the ideal family pet. They didn't even stop to let their daughter have a ride.

'Best not' said Arabella, 'she had already thrown two children that morning.'

Pixie yawned. Arabella watched with satisfaction as the family trailed away, grumbling about people who did not tell the truth in adverts. She continued to look pleased until her father stepped out of his hiding place.

'Arabella,' he said severely. Arabella looked abashed. 'What's going on?'

'Nothing,' she squeaked.

'Nothing? How can you say nothing when I've just heard you telling those people a pack of lies. Have you been saying those things to all the people who have come to see Pixie?'

Arabella started to shake her head but slowly the shake turned into a nod. She stared down at her feet.

'Now listen,' said her father, his voice tired and angry, 'you will agree to sell Pixie to the very next child who says they want her, do you hear me?'

Arabella nodded without looking up. 'I know this is hard on you, it is hard on all of us, but you will do what I tell you. The very next family. Understand?'

Arabella nodded and his voice became gentler. 'Right , good girl. Now I'm trusting you. I've got enough to do without having to check up on this sort of thing. If you don't do what I say then Pixie will have to go to an auction.'

Arabella gasped with horror, ponies often went to slaughter from auctions.

'All right,' relented her father, 'not an auction, but she must go soon.'

He turned on his heel and went back to the house. He was due to have a meeting with the accountants shortly to hear their final summing-up and was not looking forward to it.

Arabella looked at Pixie and such a lump rose in her throat that she didn't know how to swallow. She looked up at the gardener's boy who looked back at her, his face all sadness.

Arabella suddenly realised it was awful for him too; he was losing his job, all of the staff were. Oh, everything was so terrible and there was nothing she could do, there was nothing anyone could do. The gardener's boy turned to lead Pixie away to be unsaddled.

'Wait a minute. I'll do that,' said Arabella.

The boy nodded. 'Right Miss, and Miss...'

'Yes.'

'I am sorry, I'm right fond of this little animal and it must be fair breaking your heart to have to part with her.'

'Yes,' said Arabella simply, and added, 'Thank-you.'

She smiled at him. He nodded briefly and went back to the gardens. She took hold of Pixie's bridle and led her into the stable. Undoing the girth she lifted the saddle from her back and fetching the body-brush, smoothed away the saddle mark. She undid the cheek strap and gently eased the bridle off letting the bit slip from Pixie's mouth. She made a fuss of the pony, scratching her all along her back, which Pixie loved, ending up around the pony's ears. Then Arabella looped her arms round Pixie's neck and laid her face against the rough mane, enjoying the feel, the smell, the very closeness of the pony.

'This is it then,' she whispered. 'I really am going to lose you, you really are going to be sold.' The gardener's boy said she must be brokenhearted and Arabella realised he was right. It felt as if her heart had to break with the heaviness and the sorrow she felt.

She took a deep breath and looking up said, 'Please make sure the right person buys her. Someone who will be kind and not pull on her mouth or kick her sides or

make her jump things to big for her or ride her too hard.'
She added, 'I'm sorry I told those lies but I told them
for the right reasons.'

Here she stopped and thought for a minute, then added
forlornly, 'No, I didn't. I told them because I stopped
trusting you. Please forgive me.' Arabella stopped.
There was that curious sensation again. That quietness
that started in her tummy and worked all through her
until even her troubled mind felt calm and peaceful.

'All things work together for good to them that love
God,' murmured Arabella. 'I do wish you could have
given her back to me, but if you know a better way, then
okay.' Giving Pixie a final pat, Arabella left the stable.

As she made her way up the path to the house, Arabella
saw her father coming towards her with a lady and a
girl. His words came back to her: 'You are to sell Pixie
to the very next child who says they want her.' So this
is the child, thought Arabella.

As they came nearer she realised the girl had already
seen Pixie the day before. She was very keen until
Arabella told her about the pony's bad habit of rearing
at bushes and the girl had reluctantly turned away.

Arabella remembered her, too, because she was one
of the nicer ones to view Pixie. She rode well and
seemed kind. At least that part of her prayer had been
answered. Arabella stood where she was and waited
for them to come to her. Her father looked very stern
and said, 'Arabella, will you reassure Mrs Thompson
and Sarah here, that Pixie has never reared in her life?'
Arabella nodded.

'Sorry,' she whispered. Mrs Thompson smiled kindly.

'That's all right, Arabella. I understand. It must be very hard to part with Pixie.' Arabella couldn't answer and just stood there dumbly.

'I do like her,' said the girl, 'that is why we came back. She is everything I ever wanted in a pony and I will take very good care of her. Maybe you can come and see her sometimes, we don't live far away.' This was meant in a kind way but right then Arabella couldn't think about visiting Pixie after she was sold. She wanted her too much herself.

'Right,' said Arabella's father briskly. 'If you will come back to the house we can sort out the details.'

'Can I see Pixie again, please?' said Sarah.

'Of course,' said Arabella's father. He looked at Arabella, who went back into the stable followed by Pixie's new owner. Then he and Mrs Thompson went off to the house to organise payment and to make arrangements for Pixie to be transported to her new home the next day. Arabella's father was greatly relieved. His meeting with the accountants had been postponed until the following morning. They had just discovered something new amongst the piles of figures and they all looked very serious. Arabella's father feared it meant more bad news. At least the matter of the pony had been settled. The sooner she was gone now the better. Arabella had been through enough.

Sarah and Arabella stood together in the stable. Sarah was a nice girl who understood Arabella must be feeling awful, so wouldn't let herself sound as excited as she felt.

'You must come and see her when she is settled,' she said generously.

'Thank-you,' said Arabella. 'I would like that. You will be kind to her?'

'Of course, I said so.'

'She likes to be scratched behind the ears.'

'I'll remember.'

'And she likes carrots and sugar lumps, only don't give her too much sugar, it's bad for her teeth.'

'I know.'

'And don't pull on her mouth too much, she's very sensitive.'

'All right.'

'And don't try to jump her too high, she's so willing she'll have a go at anything and might be hurt.'

'I won't.'

'You will be kind to her, won't you?' said Arabella again.

'Yes, I will,' said Sarah patiently. The two girls stood beside Pixie, one suffocating with excitement and one breathless with sorrow.

Soon Mrs Thompson and Sarah were gone, payment had been made and a horse box booked for two o'clock the following afternoon to take Pixie to her new home.

Arabella went to her room, lay on her bed and wept as if her heart had been broken in two.

Chapter 17

The next morning, the Brown family sat down to breakfast. None of them felt like eating. Arabella's father chewed on toast that was as hard to swallow as cardboard. Her mother sipped black coffee and played nervously with her napkin, while Arabella stirred her cereal round and round the bowl until her father snapped, 'Will you eat that or leave the table.'

Arabella took a mouthful but found it almost impossible to swallow. The maid brought bacon and eggs, her face pale and sorrowful, she had left Cook weeping in the kitchen. Hargreaves was out giving his beloved Bentley a polish, knowing it would soon be sold and everyone in the house crept around miserably.

After breakfast, Arabella went to have one last ride on Pixie. Her father went to the study for the vital meeting with the accountants, while her mother stayed sitting at the breakfast table, not sure what to do with herself.

Arabella had told Mary the last ride would be to the vicarage, so she could say goodbye to Pixie too. Mary's family had been praying hard for Arabella and her parents, but they'd all begun to feel that God's plan was not exactly what they would have chosen it to be. Mary's father and mother knew in the long run this could only be for the best, but it was hard to see a family, who were fast becoming good friends, so unhappy.

Arabella was gone over two hours and as she rode away from the vicarage she looked back at the sad little group. She could see Mary was crying while Fred had his face buried in his mother's skirts. She rode home the long way finally turning in through the gates at the end of the drive. She couldn't believe that it was really the last time she would do this and that by the afternoon Pixie would be gone. She started towards the house.

As Arabella got nearer she could see her mother standing at the front door. She was gazing down the drive and it looked as if she was waiting for someone to arrive. When she caught sight of Arabella she put her hand to her mouth and started to run towards her.

Arabella was really worried, her mother never ran anywhere. What had happened now? She saw her mother was weeping copiously, and a coldness gripped Arabella's heart. Was there more bad news?

At last her mother reached her and stood beside Pixie, choking back the tears, trying to speak.

'What is it, Mumsy?' What's happened?'

With great difficulty her mother took control of herself, she breathed deeply for a few seconds before blurting out, 'It's all right! Everything is all right! We don't have to move after all!'

Arabella felt faint and she swayed precariously on Pixie's back. Her mother, seeing her reaction, helped her down to the ground before continuing.

'The accountants found a mistake in your father's figures, a mistake made ages ago. It seems it led to other mistakes and soon everything began to look wrong. There hasn't been a proper picture of our finances for months. No wonder he's been looking worried for so long. I told him to get a proper accountant, but no, he's always been so proud of doing the figures himself.'

Her words sounded angry but her voice was light and full of laughter and tears.

'Then at almost exactly the same time as the accountants told us this news, we received a phone call to say the company had received a huge order from abroad and so the business is safe too. Apparently Australia want half a million musical bowler hats that play *Waltzing Matilda*. Can you imagine?'

Arabella couldn't. It was all too much to take in. To go from so much sadness to so much joy in such a short time made her feel dizzy.

'We really don't have to move?'

'No we don't. In fact things aren't going to change at all.'

'One thing has changed,' said Arabella soberly.

'What's that darling?'

'Pixie is sold.'

'Oh! Well, if we give Mrs Thompson her money back she won't be sold any more.'

Arabella squealed with delight and jumped up and down with excitement; she hugged her mother who hugged her back, 'Hurry and take Pixie to the stable then come indoors, we must celebrate.'

Arabella tore round to the back of the house and down to the stable with Pixie trotting hard beside her, sometimes breaking into a canter to keep up. Arabella shouted for the gardener's boy and he came running at top speed, wondering what all the fuss was about. He was surprised to see her looking so flushed and happy and Arabella realised the staff hadn't been told the good news yet.

'Sort her out for me will you?' she threw him the reins and Pixie tossed her head startled.

'Yes Miss,' he called after Arabella, as she charged up the path towards the house. As she ran, she sang one of the songs she'd learnt in church at the top of her voice. It was full of praise and all about leaping for joy which right at that moment suited Arabella fine.

Arabella galloped into the house. She found her parents in the hall and flung herself into her father's arms.

'Isn't it wonderful, Daddy? I can't believe it's true!'

'I know, darling, I know.' He swung her round while Arabella's mother danced a little jig all on her own. Lydia and the butler came out to see what was going on and Arabella's father just had to tell them.

'Everything is all right, we aren't moving, your jobs are safe and I'm giving you all a rise.'

Lydia squealed and clapped her hands delightedly and the butler said, 'May I, on behalf of the staff, extend my heartiest felicitations, sir. This is indeed splendiferous news,' - which meant he was pleased.

The word spread like wildfire and all the staff celebrated in their own ways. Hargreaves went to give the Bentley yet another polish, the gardener drove in circles on the lawn mower with the blades up, while Cook sat at the kitchen table and cried and cried into her apron. It was a marvellous, marvellous day.

There was only one more thing to do and that was to make sure Pixie was safe. 'Daddy, can you give Mrs Thompson her money back? Mummy said you could and then Pixie won't be sold any more.' Her father stopped and went as white as a sheet.

'Oh Arabella. The money went into the bank yesterday and Mrs Thompson has Pixie's papers. There is nothing I can do; Sarah Thompson is Pixie's legal owner.'

Chapter 18

Arabella's father was on the telephone. He was calling Mrs Thompson's house to try to speak to her before she left with the horse box, but she and Sarah were already on the way.

'There's nothing we can do now but wait,' he said to Arabella, 'and hope Mrs Thompson will understand when she gets here.'

Arabella couldn't believe how things had turned out. Was she going to lose Pixie even after all this? She remembered, hopefully, how nice Sarah was and Mrs Thompson's kind smile, surely they must understand and let her have Pixie back. Then she remembered how much Sarah had loved Pixie. 'She is everything I ever wanted in a pony,' she'd said, and Arabella despaired.

The celebrations in the house were put on hold until the matter of the pony was settled. Everyone hoped desperately for a happy outcome knowing if there wasn't one, any celebrating would have a hollow ring to it.

It was time for lunch. This was going to be such a special, happy meal but now it was almost as quiet and difficult as breakfast had been. Arabella's parents knew it would be wrong to sound as happy as they felt while Arabella was so worried.

The maid served the first course which was tomato soup with tiny home-made bread rolls. Normally,

Arabella loved this but as she lifted the first spoonful to her mouth, there seemed to be a large lump in her throat which even tomato soup couldn't get past. She sat poised, staring at the spoon, then slowly put it back into the bowl.

'Excuse me,' she said softly, before getting down from the table. She left the dining room and went upstairs to her bedroom while her parents watched with concerned faces.

Arabella knew the only way forward was to pray. She remembered kneeling during the service in the cathedral and at the time wondered why she should. Now, somehow, it felt right to do so. It seemed the only way to express how she was feeling, not just about Pixie but about God himself.

She knelt by the bed, and from her heart told him how grateful she was to him for finding her, for forgiving her for all the wrong things she had done, and how she wanted to follow him always. She told him Pixie or no Pixie that she was his and nothing would change that. She thanked him for giving her family back their home and prayed that her parents would soon understand about him too, she just laid everything before him including herself. She and Jesus spent five special minutes together, before she got up feeling much, much better.

Back in the dining room, Arabella's parents were amazed to see their daughter walk back in and sit down at the dining table.

She looked at them both and smiled shyly, then quietly picked up her spoon and began to eat.

At two o'clock sharp, a horse box pulled up in front of Arabella's home. A pleasant-looking lady and an excited girl jumped from the cab and went to the front door. In the house, Arabella's father took a deep breath. He answered the door himself and greeted Mrs Thompson and Sarah warmly.

He invited them into the drawing room and they went through looking puzzled, they had expected to go straight to the stable.

Arabella and her mother were already in the drawing room waiting. They both smiled as Mrs Thompson and Sarah entered. Arabella's father didn't wait any longer but told them about the events of the morning and how things had worked out. He explained that they were no longer moving because he was no longer financially ruined and then asked bluntly if they would allow Arabella to keep Pixie. There was a long pause before Mrs Thompson answered.

'That has to be up to Sarah.' she said. 'Pixie is hers and I can't give her back to you.' They all looked at Sarah expectantly and Mrs Thompson put a comforting arm around her daughter's shoulders. Sarah looked very upset. She thought she was just going to collect her new pony and take her home, now this had happened. Her face became hard and she looked stubbornly at the floor, why should she give up such a lovely pony? She looked up ready to say no but suddenly found she couldn't. Biting her lip and with tears in her eyes, her face softened, she looked at Arabella and nodded. Arabella's heart soared.

'Sarah,' said Arabella's father, 'thank-you very, very

much.' And then to Mrs Thompson he said, 'You must be very proud of such a generous daughter.'

Mrs Thompson nodded and looked near to tears herself. He rang a small bell on a nearby table and when a maid came he ordered coffee for the adults and fizzy drinks for Arabella and Sarah. He arranged for Mrs Thompson's money to be returned to her and then they all sat together chatting. It was a little awkward at first but as the tension of the difficult moment passed they soon found things in common.

Arabella and Sarah sat across the room from one an other looking at each other shyly. Suddenly Sarah touched her mother's arm and whispered something.

'Oh, I don't think that would be a good idea at all!' her mother responded.

'But I want to,' said Sarah. Her mother shrugged.

'Could Sarah see Pixie again?'

'Are you sure you want to?' said Arabella's mother, worried it might cause the girl more hurt. Sarah nodded vigorously, so of course she was allowed.

The two girls walked together down to the stable. At first there was an awkward silence between them, neither knew what to say to the other. Finally, Arabella spoke.

'Thank-you,' she said, looking earnestly as Sarah.

'That's all right,' said Sarah sadly.

'I don't know if could have done it.'

'It was the right thing to do.'

'Yes. It's hard to do the right thing sometimes isn't it?'

Sarah nodded. 'But it helps if you know it's what God wants,' she said shyly. Arabella stopped short in amazement.

'You too?' she said wonderingly. Sarah stopped as well. The two girls looked at each other hard for a second or two, then a big smile spread across both faces and they burst out laughing with sheer pleasure as they realised ponies weren't all they had in common. Secretly, they both wanted to hug each other but as neither knew how to make the first move, they walked on.

In the stable, Sarah stroked Pixie. 'She is lovely.'

'Yes, she is,' said Arabella warmly. Then she had an idea. 'When she was yours, you said I could visit and see her sometimes. Would you like to do it the other way round? You could visit Pixie and have a ride.'

Sarah looked pleased. Arabella began to get excited. 'When you do buy your own pony maybe we could go out for a ride together, you said you didn't live far away.'

They discovered Sarah lived in the next village about three miles away, but agreed that this distance shouldn't stop them from seeing each other again.

So it was all agreed. After that celebrations began in earnest. Arabella's father threw a big party. A huge marquee was put up in the garden and he hired caterers to do the food and serve because his own staff were all invited as guests.

Cook was terribly excited and bought a new dress, she even took her apron off for the occasion.

Lots of family and friends were also invited to join the festivities. These included Mary's family, Mrs Carlton and Don and Rachel, even Mrs Thompson and Sarah came with Mr Thompson and Sarah's two younger brothers. After all, there wouldn't be so much cause to celebrate if Sarah hadn't been so generous, reasoned Arabella's father. By now Sarah was the proud owner of a beautiful nut-brown pony called Sam.

The occasion was everything Arabella's family wished it to be. Lots of fun and laughter. The invitations had said that if guests wished to bring their swimming costumes the pool would be open, and as many did there was a lot of splashing too.

After the food, Arabella's father made a speech to say how happy and grateful he was, thanking Mary's parents and the Thompsons for being specially kind and helpful. He ended by saying that he also had a feeling that someone up there - he pointed to the sky - had been looking after them.

Arabella, Sarah and Mary, standing together, all giggled with delight and Mary's parents and Sarah's parents looked knowingly at each other. It turned out they had been friends for years.

The day was one long happy blur for Arabella and as the celebrating went on into the evening she became dreamily tired. By nine at night, she and Mary and Sarah were lying on the grass their heads together, chatting away.

Sarah described Sam to them and Arabella and Mary said they couldn't wait to see him. She invited them both to spend a Saturday at her home and they were thrilled to accept. The evening wore on and the girls chatting became punctuated with yawns, eventually Sarah nodded off. Arabella and Mary talked together for a few minutes longer before falling asleep at exactly the same moment. Half an hour later, three sets of parents, all looking for their daughters, came across three girls fast asleep in the middle of the lawn. They all chuckled at the sight and Arabella's father ran to get his camera so that he could record the moment and show the girls later. Then the fathers each picked up their own daughter and gently carried them home to bed.

The following Sunday, Arabella went to church as usual. She sat with Mary and the other children but turned round often to smile and wave reassuringly at her parents who were sitting with Mary's mother, looking a little uncomfortable.

Mary's father came out of his office and walked to the pulpit. He turned to his congregation and smiled a broad smile. Everyone smiled back, even Arabella's parents. 'Lovely,' he thought. 'A nice full church, that's what I like to see.' Then with a thankful heart he announced the first hymn.